Chandler's List

A Comedy

*Have fun with this adventure!
all the best*

Lawrence M. Zaccaro

Dedication

This book is dedicated to our late mother, Marilyn F. Zaccaro, whose generosity and love helped us, her six children, remain a loving and close-knit family to this day.

Acknowledgement

Many people I know and love have contributed ideas for this work of fiction.

For my siblings, Rick, Ed, Nanc, Dan and Mike, thank you so much for the laughs while proposing ideas for the children's activities and situations in this story.

And to my children, Lauren, Kristin, Mike and Eric, thank you very much for your love and support through the years.

Love and Peace to all.

Larry Z

ISBN 9-7-986574811-8-1

Requests for information may be addressed directly to the author at zaccarolarry@gmail.com

Cover designed and illustrated by
Patrick Regan
pat123xyz.com

Chapter 1

Present Day

Brown grass and bare shrubs were on either side of the gray brick walkway that was covered with a flourishing crop of green mold. Or maybe it was algae. The cement steps leading up to the front door of the house were worn and cracked. The black iron railing was flaked with rust and badly needed painting. Remnant piles of snow were next to the steps and under the shrubs, partly covering layers of brown oak leaves that had never been moved by a rake. And the white, vinyl siding on the two story colonial house should have been spray washed two years ago, but the mold and/or algae was winning that game of turf domination as well. The black shutters around the windows looked best, only because the dirt and mold didn't show.

The front door opened quickly and Deb Chandler hurried out. A fit woman of 38, she was wearing a short, black skirt and burgundy golf shirt with a company logo stitched above the left pocket. Her brunette hair was tied up and back tightly. It was so taut, in fact, that it did not bounce as she ran down the steps.

She began talking as soon as she opened the front door.

"They've eaten but haven't done homework. Dishes aren't done. The laundry on the bed is clean. Kevin burned the floor. Text you later."

She hurried past without pausing, certainly not for a hug or kiss, scarcely glancing up.

Tom Chandler barely heard or saw her, but said passively, "Okay, thanks." Today he looked older than his 40 years. His face was pale and tired, and there were darkened circles under his cobalt blue eyes. His short, black thinning hair was streaked with gray, and he was holding a worn leather briefcase.

Tom had left the well-worn, blue Volvo wagon running in the driveway, with the driver's door open. Deb jumped in the driver's seat and slammed the door all in one motion. The car quickly backed out of their short driveway and lurched away too fast for their residential street.

Tom closed the front door behind him and set down the briefcase close to the bottom of the stairs. He trudged through the hallway into the living room.

Kevin Chandler, 13, and Kaitlyn Chandler, 10, were sitting on the beige cloth sofa. From the large, high-definition television emanated sounds of many people screaming in horror as they were attacked by flesh-eating zombies. Kevin and Kaitlyn were passively watching and did not look up to greet, or even notice Tom. Until he spoke.

"Hi guys."

Kaitlyn leapt to her feet and ran over in front of the living room windows. She pointed enthusiastically at a spot on the floor as she exclaimed with excitement, "Kevin burned the floor!"

Kevin looked up at her. "Brat!"

Tom walked across the room to the spot and looked down at the damage. "What happened?" He knelt and inspected the oak floor, and lightly fingered a branded 'KC' burned into the wood.

Kevin explained, a bit panicked, "I was seeing if my magnifying glass really would burn something, just using the sun!"

Tom sighed heavily. "Right into the floor? Really?"

Kevin cried out, "Well, I didn't know!"

Tom tried to speak calmly, "Now you know, right?"

"Yes!"

Tom looked around, assessing the condition of the rest of the room. No more apparent damage but generally cluttered, as usual. "Where's Emily?"

Kevin rolled his eyes. "Where she always is . . . upstairs doing FaceTime or something on her stupid iPhone, trying to get a boyfriend. But it's more like she's fishing without any bait. Good luck with that!"

"Kevin! Knock that off!"

The landline phone buzzed, and Kaitlyn ran past Tom to answer the handset that was hanging just inside the kitchen. He didn't bother trying to stop her, since no important calls ever came through the landline anymore.

"Hello?" Kaitlyn said.

On the other end, a friendly woman's voice said, "Hello, this is a courtesy call from Community Dental reminding Thomas Chandler of his appointment . . ."

Kaitlyn quickly interrupted, saying, "I'm sorry, we don't accept courtesy calls." And she hung up the handset.

Tom was walking toward the kitchen, and watched her passively, until she spoke and hung up. "'We don't accept courtesy calls?' Who was that?" Tom asked.

Kaitlyn said, "A dentist or something. You and Mom said no courtesy calls."

It took a second for what she said to register with him. "No, we said, no solicitor calls. Solicitation, sales calls. Courtesy calls are okay."

Kaitlyn sheepish said, "Oh. Sorry."

Tom said dismissively, "That's okay, I know when my appointment is."

Intense screaming on the television drew Tom's concerned attention. Not even bothering to ask what show they were watching, he said, "Can you guys get going on your homework?"

Kevin's gaze now did not veer from the television. "As soon as this one is over."

Tom said noncommittally, "Let me know if you need help with any of it."

He walked out of the living room into the kitchen. If possible, his mood and posture slumped even more. The kitchen table was covered with papers, books and assorted clutter, certainly stuff that had nothing to do with eating a meal. Dirty dishes filled the sink, some crusted with food from two days ago. Plastic containers full of leftovers were piled onto the jammed counter.

There was a scribbled note there which read, 'Heat up what want put away rest sorry didn't get dish.'

He surveyed the state of the kitchen and sighed with resignation.

Tom was still awake in bed when Deb walked into their room at 11:45. One lamp on one night stand inadequately lit the modest furnishings and cramped space. Without even a hello, she said, "The engine warning light came on when I was driving home." She sat in the chair in the corner of the room and started to get undressed, flipping her shoes off in the faint direction of the closet.

Tom rolled over, and also without a hello, asked, "The little yellow engine symbol, or the big square red one?"

"The red one started flashing, and the message screen said, 'stop driving immediately.'"

"Did you stop driving?"

"Of course not! It's almost midnight!"

Tom sighed heavily. "How did the engine sound?"

"It ran rough, but it kept going. Oh, and now there is a message, 'multiple bulb failure.' One of the headlights went out, too."

"Shit. I'll take that car to work tomorrow and bring it to the shop at lunch."

She pulled her work blouse over her head, and unclipped her bra, but Tom didn't express the slightest interest in looking at her exposed, well-proportioned body. She said, "It's got 237,000 miles on it. We're going to have to get something else soon. It's going to break down when we have the kids in the car. That'll just be dangerous."

"Oh, by the way, we don't have goldfish anymore. The last one was floating dead in the bowl."

"I'm not surprised. I'm sure the water never got changed. I never think about it."

Tom said, "It wasn't the water. The poor thing had a neat little row of four holes in its side. That just so happen to line up exactly with the holes a fork would make."

She looked up at him. "One of the kids stabbed their last goldfish with a fork?"

"No one admitted it, but I'll bet you a bazillion dollars it was your son."

She looked at him with dagger eyes. "Right. Only my son would do that. You're an ass." She threw off the rest of her clothes. "Doesn't matter. It's just one less thing to take care of."

Tom didn't say anything but just laid down, facing away from her side of the bed. He pulled the blanket up over his shoulders.

"I'm taking a shower." She said very sarcastically, "Don't bother waiting up for me. Nothing is going to 'happen' tonight."

In the distance, dozens of magnificent black stallions, each carrying a leather-armored, long-haired soldier, were galloping over the grass and scrub brush of the Scottish moors. The pounding of the horses' hooves was distant, muffled, but inexorably growing louder.

Closer the stallions came, piercing the mist. The soldiers were yelling but their war cries were drowned out by the thundering on the ground. The stallions' manes were flying, swirling as they galloped. Hooves pulverized the saturated dirt, flecks of mud and twigs churning in a swirling debris cloud. The frenzied breath of the soldiers and horses trailed behind them, vanishing into the misty shroud that hung in the air.

The pounding of the hooves grew louder, louder, a rhythmic clamoring cadence.

The horses passed by on all sides as the rhythmic pounding escalated to an all-consuming, thunderous roar.

Deb's eyes sprung open as she suddenly jumped awake. The pounding of hooves had blended smoothly into Tom's rhythmic snoring, directly in her ear. Her head was on her pillow with Tom laying on his back behind her.

In an annoyed whisper, Deb said, "Hey, Braveheart, roll over."

Tom's snoring abruptly stopped with stuttered breathes, and he emitted a puzzled groan. He rolled to his other side, facing away from Deb.

She sighed with exasperation, gruffly adjusted her pillow and slammed down her head, eyes wide open and annoyed.

Chapter 2

On the shore of the Thames River in New London, not the 'Tems' in regular London, stood a complex of three cement, brick and glass office towers, six stories high. An engraved brass plaque near the entrance at ground level read:

SOEL International Headquarters

Inside her small, starkly furnished office sat Ashley Rogers, a striking woman of 36, with long, luxurious red hair and dazzling green eyes. She was dressed in a conservative business suit, behind a desk cluttered with folders, papers and one overmatched laptop.

She said politely, "It's trail of ownership protocol. You know it's strict policy."

Tom was leaning forward in the chair across the desk, not very happy. He said firmly, "The brass thread borer was taken out of use for seventy-two hours. Because one of the pipe-fitters didn't know where the ownership form was. It set the project back an entire week. Another week! On top of the months delay already!"

Ashley agreed, "I know. I'm catching hell for it."

He said with annoyance, "Those spec sheets won't be delivered on time. And it's got nothing to do with anyone's work quality. Just an f-ing form being in the wrong folder or something."

"Tom, we all have to deal with management hassles. I'll bring it up at the next directors meeting, but in the meantime, work on things you can control."

Resigned, Tom leaned back in the chair, folding his arms and looking out the window. He absently said, "Pour honey in my ass and tie me to a fire ant hill."

Ashley said sarcastically, "The good news is, they're eliminating all overtime."

He turned and looked hard at her. "Seriously? When is that starting?"

"The first of the month. I just left that meeting. And yes, that will make it all but impossible to meet timelines on our projects."

Tom muttered, "Shit," and said, "oh, for the love of . . ."

Ashley laughed sincerely, "The actual good news is, you can't be here more than forty hours a week, even if you want to."

That evening, in the Chandlers' master bedroom, Tom was sitting in bed wearing a white tee shirt. Deb was still in her work uniform on the edge of the bed. Neither one looked particularly happy.

Tom continued, "Ashley told me today. We can't even be approved for five hours of OT anymore."

Deb snapped, "Ashley, that red-headed slut?"

Tom replied, "She's not a slut. She's married with two kids."

"How else did she get the supervisor job instead of you?"

Tom's voice was inadvertently raising in volume. "You mean, besides the fact that our CEO announced to the world, 'we will make it a priority of this company to fill the ranks of management with women and minorities?' Is any part of that unclear?"

Deb said, "Like I said, a slut."

"She works hard." And then he added, "Yeah, she plays the management crap-a-roni game. And, yeah, she looks good doing it."

Deb didn't let up, and said, "Maybe you can sleep with her and then get that overdue promotion."

"Don't even start with that bullshit again."

Deb looked away and shook her head. "So all the hours I put in at work won't be worth a thing."

"No need to sugar-coat it like that, Pollyanna. And the car repair is two timing valve solenoids, or some random parts I've never heard of. That will be a cool fifteen hundred."

Deb looked back at him. "Oh, are we playing the Glad Game? I hadn't noticed, since everything coming out of your mouth is such happy news. This is a little different from the last time I played."

Tom tried to revitalize a win-win synergy for the primary stakeholders. "I'll be making two hundred less a week, however you want to look at it. But I'll be home just after four. I can help more with meals, and house and kid stuff."

Deb snapped sarcastically, "Like you help with cleaning now?"

"I've been doing what I can."

Deb's voice rose in volume even more. "I actually tried to clean today. Here's a hall-of-famer. There were cobwebs on the vacuum cleaner. Cobwebs on the vacuum! Not a good sign we're keeping up with cleaning." She got up from the bed. "Whatever. It doesn't matter anymore. I'm taking a shower."

Twenty minutes later, Deb had just crawled into bed. Tom was still awake and had been lying on his side, facing the other way. He rolled over and moved toward her immediately. Looking for affection, he reached for her under the blanket.

Deb noticeably and immediately recoiled from his touch.

Tom quickly pulled back his hand. "That was warm and fuzzy. Hey, don't worry, my leprosy is in remission."

Deb said bitterly, "I just worked all night, for negative income. I'm not exactly in the mood."

"Not in the mood, again, you mean. What's it been, two weeks?" He rolled over and laid on his side, facing away from her.

"Don't give me that. I'm on my feet six straight hours, four nights a week. The rest of my life is house, kids and errands. I'm tired."

Tom lifted his head. "I haven't exactly been sprawled out on the couch like a relaxed jellyfish watching The View for the last fifteen years."

She growled, "Go to hell."

"I'm already there," he said quickly. He thought for a second then said, "And no need to worry about actually getting to hell. Our ticket there is already prepaid and punched. When you made the kids all go to confession."

Deb was incredulous. "What? That was for First Communion! You're bringing up that again? Jesus Christ!"

Tom recounted the story in his head, but almost forgot he was saying it out loud. "Kevin had no idea what to say. They sort of taught him the Ten Commandments. I guess he knew he hadn't killed anyone. He didn't know what 'covet' or 'adultery' meant, so he just picked a random one to have something to confess. Eight years old, and he confessed to committing adultery! Adultery! And not just once, but six times!"

Sometimes Deb found that story amusing, but she wasn't laughing now. "The pathetic thing was, Father Dunn yelled at him because he committed adultery! Not because he just made up some ridiculous answer!"

"I'll never forget the image of him walking back from the altar right after getting his First Communion. Taking the host out of his mouth and putting it in his pocket, because it tasted gross! The Body of Christ in his pocket!"

"I guess we should have prepared him more for that."

"He'll never recover. No wonder he does the things he does." Tom paused, then, "And what was with his hair today?"

Deb shook her head. "He decided he didn't like his haircut, so he tried to cut his own."

"Jesus, what a disaster. It looks like a blindfolded lumberjack did it with a chainsaw. I'll take him to the barbershop to see if they can fix it." Tom sighed. "He's almost for sure going to need counseling."

For a couple minutes, a gaunt, tense silence hung in the room as they contemplated that future prospect.

Tom finally muttered, "This is quite a life we've carved out for ourselves."

Deb was laying on her side, facing away from him. "Don't get me started. If I describe everything that's wrong, I'll be talking until Rapture. Which can't come soon enough."

Tom said seriously, almost as a challenge, "Go ahead. I'm not going anywhere, start talking." He thought a second. "Better yet, make a list."

Deb rolled back over to face him. "Write down what's wrong with our life? Are you f-ing kidding me?"

"We both know that a counselor isn't going to work for us. So let's make a list . . . okay, make a list with two columns. For Pollyanna, good things on one side, and for me, bad things on the other. I'll do the same. Then we can go out somewhere, like a bar or somewhere, and talk about it all. Maybe we can actually work through some stuff, figure out some answers. And build on the good things."

She shook her head and laid back down. "Boy, does that sound like a rip-roaring good time."

"We can't keep going like this. Maybe it'll help."

Deb said bitterly, "You're right, we can't keep this up, and a counselor won't help. But sure, I'll make a list. And then we can go out and fight . . . I mean, talk about it." Deb roughly fluffed her pillow and pulled up the covers. Finally, she said, "The best part is, it'll be our first date in months."

Chapter 3

TEN AND A HALF YEARS EARLIER

Five-year-old Emily, pretty with long brown hair, peered into the window of the huge Mercury station wagon. It was dark in the old detached garage, so she couldn't see inside the car very well. She tentatively pulled the handle of the driver's door. It popped open.

"Em-wee! Don't!" chirped Kevin, two, who was right behind her. "That's Grammy's car!"

"Quiet, brat! I'm not hurting anything!" With some effort, she pushed open the heavy door and climbed up into the seat behind the steering wheel.

Kevin cried, "Let me in!" After several tries, without help from Emily, he crawled in and scrambled over her to the passenger's seat.

Emily sat with both hands on the wheel, yanking it back and forth as if driving. She imitated the putt-putt of an engine with her tongue and lips. Then she decided to try and reach the pedals by extending her legs, but couldn't quite reach.

Kevin saw that her legs almost reached the floor. Since his legs didn't come close, he was very impressed that hers were so long. He exclaimed, "Wow, you're almost married!"

Emily rolled her eyes and continued to 'drive.'

As Kevin was anxiously waiting to take his turn behind the wheel, he noticed the knobs and controls on the dashboard. He climbed down to the floor and started pulling and poking the intriguing contraptions. He pulled heat and AC levers back and forth, and turned radio dials. Then he pushed in the cigarette lighter. He and Emily were both surprised when it stayed locked inward with a click.

Emily said, "You're going to break something!" After a few seconds, the lighter popped out with a loud clunk. She grabbed for it before he could, and yanked it out of the dashboard. She was surprised to see the glowing, bright orange coil. Peering at it, she could feel its radiating heat.

Kevin cried, "Lemme see!"

Emily's eyes narrow, and with a mischievous grin, turned the business end of the lighter toward Kevin, and said, "Pretty! Touch it!"

Kevin hesitated at first, but reached out for the hot coil with his little index finger. Emily quickly moved the lighter the last inch to close the gap. With a sizzle, a small puff of smoke, and a horrible smell, the tip of Kevin's finger was burned.

He screeched, grabbed his hand and immediately started crying.

Emily's mischievous grin quickly vanished, and she realized doing that was not such a good idea. She pushed the lighter back in the outlet and said, "We better go tell Mommy and Daddy."

Deb's mother, Lynn, who looked like a more care-worn version of Deb, was thirty-five years older but in great shape physically. She gently applied ointment to the tip of Kevin's finger and wrapped a Band-Aid around it carefully. "You two should be a little more careful next time," she said kindly. They were in a modestly furnished and extremely worn kitchen. The cabinets fit poorly into the spaces on the walls, as if the required measurements had nothing to do with their actual dimensions. Their wood stain had faded badly. And the linoleum floor was worn through to plywood in spots, and permanently stained.

"Thanks, Mom," said Deb, standing nearby. She was wearing a loose-fitting summer maternity dress, since she was six months pregnant. Her brunette hair hung half way down her back and was tied in a loose ponytail. She looked youthful and radiant. Deb said to Emily, who was also watching the medical procedure with concern, "You two stay in the house now. You shouldn't be wandering around out there. We all need to go to bed early."

Emily whined, "We haven't seen Grammy's yard!"

Deb said, "I know, but we have to leave early in the morning. Dad wants to get to Connecticut before dinner tomorrow."

"I've never been to Ohio! All we saw is our car and a room, and Grammy's car, and another room!"

Lynn finished with Kevin and said, "There, that should feel better." She looked up at Deb. "The kids would love seeing the yard! I have nine kinds of fruits and vegetables! Raspberries, asparagus, chives, rhubarb. This house is a gold mine!"

"I know, Mom, but our schedule for moving is pretty tight."

Tom, 29, walked into the kitchen. His hair was black without a hint of gray, and very neatly trimmed. In business casual clothes, he looked happy and energetic. He said, "Lynn, do you have bottled water in fridge? I used our last one on the road today."

"No, dear, but you could have tap water, and I think there's ice in the freezer."

"Okay, thanks." Searching for a glass, Tom opened the cabinet nearest the sink. There were random old coffee cups, shoe boxes loaded with papers, small random medicine vials and various other containers, but no glasses. Tom looked in the next cabinet over, and found it was also full of assorted stuff, but nothing resembling a glass. He grabbed the largest coffee mug he could find.

Deb said to Kevin and Emily, "Why don't you guys go up to our room. Grammy said we'll have our own little TV up there! You can watch anything you want for a while."

Emily squealed with delight and ran out of the kitchen. Kevin was still trying to regroup from his burned finger, and after a moment's delay, slowly followed her out.

Tom stepped to the kitchen sink in front of a small window, noticing three medicine vials upside down on the window sill. As he was running tap water into his coffee mug, and saw immediately the water was cloudy. His face crinkled in disgust and he smelled it. Though not with a confirmed odor, he let the water run for a while before filling the mug. He carried the water across the room to the freezer, above the very old refrigerator. In order to pull out the only ice cube tray, he had to dig under, and completely rearrange, piles of random, frozen objects. Most of the items were coated with a thick frozen, purple smear. He was able to trace the purple to a bag of very old blueberries. It had long ago been stored in there, at some point had leaked badly, and then had not been disturbed for possibly years.

The ice cube tray was not stained purple. But when he was finally able to dislodge it from the clutter, he found the ice was so old, it was coated with a greenish-black entity. He couldn't tell if it was mold, or dirt, or maybe something else that had leaked. He didn't want to know. After putting everything back into the freezer, he closed the door, and decided lukewarm water would be fine.

After taking a sip, and almost gagging from the hard, metallic taste, he looked in the refrigerator for anything else that was light and potable. There was milk, V-8 and orange juice, so he decided the latter would be just swell. As he pulled out the bottle of juice, he noticed two styrofoam carryout food containers. Both had the word 'NEW' written on them. As he was pouring his juice into his coffee mug, he asked, "Lynn, what are these containers in the fridge that say, 'new?'"

Lynn beamed with pride. "That's my system I developed! Whenever I get a leftover meal from a restaurant, I write 'new' on them so I'll know which ones are the freshest!"

Tom started to speak, but quickly caught himself. He then asked, "And the upside-down medicines on the window sill?"

"Oh yes, I must tell you. When I take my medicines every day, I turn them upside down so I'll know I've taken them!" She was so proud she had devised this simple yet brilliant system.

Tom hesitated again, but then asked, "Don't you have one of those daily pill boxes you could fill every week? Wouldn't that work better to keep track of your pills?"

"Oh, I would never remember to fill a big box like that! My system is so much better."

They were leaving in the morning, so instead of trying to explain things to her, Tom just let it go. But he did ask, "Did you know your ice cubes look kind of old?"

"Oh, I never use ice. It hurts my teeth."

Tom put the juice bottle back in the refrigerator, thinking, that explains a lot about the state of the freezer contents.

Later, after the kids were finally settled in bed upstairs, Tom, Deb and Lynn were sitting at the dining room table chatting and catching up a bit.

"How long did it take you to drive from Denver?" Lynn asked, sipping a cup of tea.

Deb said, "We stayed in Missouri last night, just west of St. Louis. Probably about eleven hours on the road each day."

Tom added, "We stayed in a hotel. SOEL, my new company in Connecticut, is paying for most of the move!"

Lynn said, "It's nice to see you all, I haven't seen the kids since last year!"

"Thanks for putting up with us for the night!" said Tom.

Deb asked her, "I know it's been ten years since Dad died, but how are you getting on? Isn't this house and yard too much to take care of?"

"Oh, I would never move! This house is a gold mine, with all the fruits and vegetables in the yard! Asparagus, raspberries, rhubarb, chives!"

Tom looked at the film of dust on the window sill closest to the table. Not only hadn't the window been cleaned, probably for years, it looked like it had not been opened in that long. And it looked likely that it could not be opened, even if they had tried.

Lynn added, "I do have Betty's boyfriend mow the lawn for me. He has one of those big riding lawn mowers."

"That's at least something," said Deb, "good."

"And Betty cleans the house twice a month."

Tom's eyes got very wide but he didn't say anything.

Lynn said, "I was hoping you would move closer to here. Connecticut is just as far away as Denver!"

Tom said, "Well, it's about 550 miles to our new house. Denver is about thirteen hundred miles from here."

"Oh, well, it's still far. Why are you leaving Colorado?"

"My job there depended on grant money for design research," said Tom. "Raising the kids, having to worry about grant renewals every two years, was getting too stressful. SOEL has huge government contracts in place for at least another ten years. And since I grew up in Massachusetts, I've always been kind of a New Englander at heart."

Lynn hadn't really heard him, zoning out and not following as soon as he used big words, like 'grant money.' "Won't that be nice," was all she said.

Deb said, "We're excited about getting settled in a new area before the kids start school! And before the baby gets here!"

Lynn was looking away and asked Deb, "What ever happened to Donald? I always liked him."

Tom almost burst out laughing but he let Deb answer. "Mom, we broke up eight years ago. Tom and I have been married for over six years."

"Oh, right, right." Then she asked, a bit defensively, "But why did you break up with Donald?"

Reluctantly, Deb told the story again. "You might remember, though he was nice, he wasn't the smartest guy around. I was pretty sure we weren't going to stay together. He and I were discussing that very thing one day, and he wanted to know why, what was wrong? I said, 'Well, I like to read, but you don't.' And his immediate response was, 'I don't mind that you like to read!' That was the clincher for me. He kind of just didn't get it."

Again, the story didn't really register with Lynn. She smiled passively and said nothing.

Tom and Deb made eye contact and smiled. Nothing really needed to be said. It was great that Emily and Kevin could connect with their grandmother, even if only for a day. But nothing that she said could be taken seriously, and certainly wasn't anything to worry about.

Emily and Kevin were asleep on small mattresses on the floor to one side of the small bedroom upstairs. Tom and Deb had pushed together two small twin beds, without frames or headboards. Though neither of them were overweight, or bigger than average size, both mattresses sagged badly in the middle. Tom rolled to one side, to the other, then settled for lying on his back.

The room was stifling hot and stagnant, with no fan, and certainly no air conditioning.

Deb was lying on her side, watching him shift positions. She smiled and whispered gently, "It's just for one night."

"I know. I just hope I can stand up straight in the morning."
He tried to get more comfortable. "Was this your bed when you
were a kid?"

"I think it was, actually."

"I feel like I'm sleeping on a slab of Silly Putty."

Tom laid still with his eyes wide open for a minute. He
noticed the small awning window in the room. Though it was
open as far as it could be cranked, the small gap supplied no
cooling capacity of any kind. Then something else occurred to
him, and he whispered to Deb, "That window cannot possibly be
up to building code laws for fire egress. That is actually very
disturbing."

"Repeat the mantra, 'just for one night, just for one night.'
Or maybe try that immortal line from Titanic, 'it'll all be over
soon, it'll all be over soon.'"

"Right, got it. Is your mom all right? It seems like her
memory and organization have gotten a lot worse. The way she
keeps track of her medicines and other stuff. It's a bit
unsettling."

"It does seem like she's gotten worse. She's still maintaining
the whole house and yard on her own, though."

"I guess we can't worry about that now." He turned and
smiled at her. "We're off on our own new adventure."

She whispered, "We certainly are. Good night, Chandler.
Thanks for being patient with her. I love you."

"I love you too."

Chapter 4

The living room was completely empty, no furniture, no curtains, with bare walls freshly painted in light blue. The glistening, newly surfaced, hardwood floors were illuminated with bright patches of sunlight streaming through spotlessly clean windows. Even the wooden dividers, giving the windows a colonial look with true divided lites, were freshly painted.

Suddenly, a small pink and white soccer ball flew across the room, smacked the wall in the corner and ricocheted off a window. One of the glass lites cracked with an audible ticking sound, a single hairline break appearing across one corner.

Emily ran into the room to retrieve the ball. She was holding a Rubik's cube in one hand and quickly corralled the ball and held it under her foot. When she looked up, she saw the crack in the glass and guiltily checked behind her for witnesses.

A few seconds later, Kevin scurried in, trying to keep up with her. "Em-wee, wait for me! Give me a turn! Lemme try Daddy's barbie cube!" The Band-Aid was still on his index finger.

Emily was annoyed. "Can't you leave me alone for one second?"

"My turn! Lemme try!"

Before he entered the room, Tom called, "Guys, don't kick the ball in our new house!" He walked in a few seconds later.

He asked Emily, "Did something break? I thought I heard something. What happened?"

She looked very guilty but said, "Nothing! What could've happened?"

Tom looked around the room and didn't see anything obvious.

Emily continued, "Anyway, there's nothing in here to break!"

Tom let it go and said enthusiastically, "So what do you guys think of our new house? Wait until you see the back yard!"

Emily was looking around, skeptical, and said, "Where's all our stuff?"

"The moving truck is supposed to come tomorrow. We'll stay in the hotel a few nights until the house is ready."

She was now excited. "Oh, yeah, another hotel! With a pool!"

Tom added, "Mom packed our suits on top so we can get them out easily."

Deb said from the front hall, "They're right in my suitcase." She walked in slowly, wearing a different flowered, maternity dress. She stopped and stretched her back with her hands on her hips, groaning quietly. "After last night in those beds, and the drive today, it feels good to be out of the car."

Emily asked impatiently, "When can we go to the hotel?"

Kevin chirped, "I wanna splash in the pool!"

"In a little while," said Tom, "I need to check a few things here first."

With genuine excitement, Deb said to Emily and Kevin, "Why don't you two go upstairs and find your rooms. You remember we talked about which ones were for who, right?"

Squealing with delight, Emily and Kevin ran out of the room and pounded up the hardwood stairs, making an amazing amount of noise for two small children. Their footfalls echoed in the empty house, and soon excited cries of discovery could be heard upstairs.

Deb casually strolled around the room. She inspected the wood trim, the painted walls, the stained hardwood floors. She walked to the windows, fingered the wood dividers and sills thoughtfully, noticing a small crack in one of the window lites.

Out the window was the large back yard with a well-maintained lawn, though the grass needed moving now.

Flowering plants, including dozens of orange day lilies in full bloom, lined the wood stockade fence bordering the entire yard.

Tom walked over and lightly put his hand on her shoulder. She turned and beamed up at him.

He asked expectantly, "What do you think? Will this work?"

She smiled, "Ya done good, Chandler. It all looks great."

They fully embraced in a deep and lingering kiss.

While waiting for their furniture and belongings to be delivered to their new house, the Chandlers stayed at the Holiday Inn in Mystic. Emily and Kevin had spent every allowable minute in the pool and had finally crashed and burned. Both were now asleep in random, uncomfortable-looking positions in one of the queen beds in the room. Kevin's thumb was still in his mouth, hanging open slightly.

In the other bed, Tom was sitting up, in boxers and a tee shirt, reading pages in a three-ringed binder. Deb was lying on her side next to him, wearing a loose nightdress, her arm draped over his thighs. They were silent and the only sound was the low hum of the window air conditioner.

Deb rolled over slowly, looked at the kids, then turned back to Tom. She said quietly, "They're finally asleep."

"The pool sure wore them out."

Deb glanced at the binder he was reading and teased, "Getting nervous?"

"About my big first day of work? You mean, just because I've moved my very young family two thousand miles to a completely unknown state and job and everyone is completely relying on me for their life and livelihood? What's there to be nervous about?"

She smiled and patted his thigh. "Oh good, I was hoping this would be no big deal for you." Then she whispered, "Seriously, this is good timing, before the kids start school full time."

"It'd be tough for them to move away from friends if they were even a couple years older. Especially for Em."

"I sure know that. It happened to me when I was a kid. I don't want it to happen to them."

"Hopefully we can get settled, put down roots, and they can grow up New Englanders." He smiled and looked away from his reading. "And I'm looking forward to following the sports teams closer. That's the real reason we're moving here. It is the most important business."

She laughed quietly, and then propped herself up. After looking at his binder for a second, she then watched him read. "What're you studying?"

"Specs on one of my projects."

"Aren't you sleepy after the long day of driving?"

"Not really. I just want to get a head start on tomorrow."

"Good idea." Deb smiled up at him and extended her arm back over his legs. She started caressing one thigh, then the other. Soon her hand moved up under one leg of his boxers. He looked under the binder and watched her hand moving under his shorts. She said, "Do you have to keep reading?"

Tom feigned mild annoyance. "Uh, in case you haven't noticed, our offspring are in the next bed, a few feet away."

"And how do you think they got here in the first place?"

He said, "You're bad."

"Want me to be even worse?"

Tom hesitated and then relented, "Uh, sure."

Quietly, Tom closed the binder and set it aside. Deb rolled over, moving her belly with effort, so her backside was facing him. She reached under her nightdress and slid off her panties. Tom quietly slid down on his side against her and pulled the sheet up over both of them. He put his arm over her and kissed her gently on the back of the neck.

She groaned quietly, ever so softly, and closed her eyes.

Chapter 5

In the mostly full parking lot on a hazy, hot morning, the worn Ford Windstar drove down one lane and pulled into an empty space. Tom climbed out, wearing a jacket and tie. He was carrying a brand new leather briefcase, and walked between rows of parked cars.

Across the street was a complex of faded concrete and glass buildings, much older than those at the New London site. Tom opened the front door under a large sign that read:

Strategic Operations Engineering & Licensing, Inc

Jack Morton was 43, heavy and balding, in a white shirt that was much too tight for his bulbous body. His small, antiquated office was uncluttered and spotlessly clean. His head was back, mouth open, eyes closed, and he was snoring audibly. Occasionally he gasped for air, his sleep apnea breaking up this morning nap.

A knock on his office door caused him to snort loudly and jump awake. He blinked, leaned forward and stood awkwardly. In a raspy voice he said, "Come in."

The door opened and Tom entered, escorted by Christine Packer, a professional-looking, attractive secretary in her thirties.

Christine said, "Jack, you remember Tom Chandler."

Morton extended a hand and walked around his desk. "Great to see you again, Tom. Welcome aboard."

Tom was genuinely excited and said, "Thanks. It's great to finally be here, and actually be ready to go."

Christine said, "I'll leave you two. If you need anything, just buzz me."

Morton turned to her, "Thanks, Christine." He waited until the office door closed behind her, then turned to Tom. With a wide grin he said, "Yeah, I'd like to buzz her."

Tom was surprised by that comment and looked a bit stunned.

Morton motioned for Tom to take a seat. "You got signed in with security and got your badge? How was parking?"

Tom shrugged. "No problem, it all went well. Thanks."

"That could change soon. There's been so much hiring, we may need to start parking remotely and take a shuttle to the site. I get here at six every morning so I can get a close spot."

"A lot of hiring is a good thing."

Morton changed his tone. "Hey, listen, I've got to take you right to your cubicle and leave you with Chuck and Eric. Just so you're not surprised, Eric is Indian. That's dot Indian, not feather Indian." He chuckled nervously. "But don't worry, he's not a terrorist."

Tom was again surprised by what Morton said, for several reasons. He only asked about one thing, however. "Cubicle? At the last interview, didn't you say offices, or maybe shared offices?"

"That's all changing, too. They're redoing this building into almost all open space and cubicles. And the new complex in New London, that we'll be moving to eventually, will be open space. It's the growing trend in business space planning. Packing in as many people as possible. Like those rats in the overcrowding experiment."

Tom was rapidly having his initial excitement beat out of him. "I'm not familiar with that study. What happened to the rats?"

"Rampant violence, insanity, cannibalism."

Tom dismissively said, "That doesn't sound like it would be a good work environment."

Morton apologized, "Well, I got called to a meeting earlier, so I've got to get going. We need to address a 5-S violation. So I'll catch you this afternoon."

Genuinely confused, Tom asked, "Five S?"

"We'll get to all that." Morton laughed out loud. "You will know, all too soon, everything there is to know about 5-S. And you'll never recover. My desk wouldn't be this organized without it."

Tom was even more confused. "Oh . . . kay. I've got a meeting at ten with HR anyway. Benefits and stuff."

Morton stood and said, "I'll get you up to the fourth floor."

A few hours later, Tom was sitting in the SOEL Headquarters cafeteria. The large, open room was saturated with conversation and cafeteria noises. A hundred tables were all fully seated.

At one of the tables, Tom was sitting between Eric Pillai, in his late twenties, and Chuck Kurtz, in his early forties. Chuck was a tired, thin man with heavily graying hair, looking older than his numerical age. Half eaten meals were on their trays as they continued their conversation.

Eric asked, "Did HR have anything useful to say?"

Tom finished chewing and said, "Not too much I didn't know already. I chose health and dental insurance plans and 401K options. Seems like pretty good benefits"

Chuck piped in, "The 401K is the best thing about working at this place. Mine is pretty respectable now. Mounting into high six figures after twenty years."

Tom nodded, pleased to hear that. He asked Eric, "What do you think is the best thing about working here?"

Eric said immediately, "Ashley. Have you met her yet?"

Tom thought a second, "I don't think so."

Eric laughed, "Then you haven't. You'd remember. A couple cubes down from us. I doubt there's ever been a better looking engineer in the whole history of forever." Then he smiled and asked Tom, "Hey, what happened when Pinocchio met Ashley?"

Chuck piped in, "He wanted to be a real boy?"

Eric laughed, "No, but that probably happened, too. Nope, but it is well documented, he got a woody."

Tom smiled but did not comment and tried to change the subject. "What do you guys make of Jack? He seems kind of stressed out."

Eric laughed again, "You mean Snore-tin' Morton?"

Tom asked with hesitation, "You mean, like snorting cocaine?"

Eric clarified, "No, like snoring. He gets here before any of us. That looks good to management and he'll tell you it's for better parking and to get more work done. But then he just sleeps in his office. As much as he can get away with."

Chuck was chewing, and added, without looking up, "Every morning, all morning. We can usually hear his snoring all the way down at our cubicles."

Eric said, "He should start drinking coffee. Not sure why he doesn't, but it would help him. Did they teach you the company motto yet?"

Tom tried to recall, "Something about creative design for the world's security?"

Eric flashed air quotes and said, "No, not that HR crap. It's really, 'Lose your soul at SOEL.' That is the true motto."

Tom looked away. "HR didn't tell me that one. Go figure."

Tom exhaled quietly in exasperation and didn't ask anything else. He looked down at his food and ate quietly unless Eric or Chuck started new conversations. His eyes were wide and he was a bit shell-shocked.

The noise in the crowded children's pizza restaurant was carnival-like and overwhelming. The beeping of video games, and children screeching and laughing echoed and vibrated across the room. Most tables were full of families, and waitresses moved gingerly to and fro, between tables of customers.

The Chandler family was seated at a long table shared with other families. Kevin was standing on his chair, talking loudly to the family immediately to their right.

Deb looked over with concern and called out, "Kevin, honey, don't bother that family!"

Kevin turned to her, a bit incredulous, and said, "Don't worry, Mommy, everybody likes me!"

Emily called, above the noise, "Where's our pizza?"

Deb said, "They're ordered, sweetie. They'll be out soon."

Kevin pointed across the room. "Look! Chucking Cheese!"

The giant mouse mascot was a few tables down, visiting a birthday party. The kids at that table were all excited and cheering.

Deb leaned over to Tom and said, "There's a career opportunity for me. Dress like a giant rat and be worshipped by children."

Tom was staring into space, preoccupied, not listening to her, and seemingly not hearing the chaos all around them.

Deb talked louder so the kids could hear. "Did you guys ask Daddy about his first day of work?"

Emily asked, "Was it fun, Daddy?"

Tom heard his name and was brought back to the room. "Hmm? Oh, sure, sure, it was fine."

Emily also asked, "Was everyone nice?"

When Tom didn't answer right away, Deb asked him, "How's your office? Can you see Long Island Sound from the window?"

Tom answered quickly and halfheartedly. "It's fine. But I think I'd rather hear what you guys did today."

Emily chimed, "The aquarium! The penguins are so cute!"

Kevin, still standing on his chair, piped in, "Quins! Quins! And peanut butter and jellyfish!"

Emily added, "And there were Nemo fish. And black and white clown fish in the same tank. Mom said they were called mime fish."

Deb was quiet, watching Tom very closely, with a bit of concern.

Emily and Kevin were asleep in their same bed back at the hotel, again exhausted from overstimulation and new experiences. Tom and Deb were sitting on the edge of their bed, talking quietly.

As Deb tenderly rubbed his back under his tee shirt, she asked, "Really? No office?"

Tom said quietly, "A cubicle, right in the middle of a cluster of a hundred more."

"And that cluster of cubicles includes all those juvenile colleagues?"

Tom tried to make light of it. "It looks like I'll be working with Dr. Howard, Dr. Fine, Dr. Howard."

She tried to comfort him more. "There's probably a lot of nice people you haven't met yet."

"At the university in Denver, they were at least polite and professional. These guys had one crude comment after another. I'm not a prude or anything, but at least a hint of professionalism is worth something at work."

"Dot Indian, not feather Indian. That's a classic. Never heard that one. I wonder if the census will use that designation next time."

"And my boss said that! A supervising engineer, not some welder in the shipyard! It was a little like a slap in the face."

Deb stopped rubbing and patted his back under his tee shirt. "You know what I think? You're too good to get swept up in that stuff."

Tom chuckled, "It's like NASA meets the Keystone Cops."

"Concentrate on the work. Bury yourself in your projects. Then come home and be with your loving family at night."

Tom considered that. "You're right. I came here to do the engineering, and build a stable career, not be one of the guys."

Deb added, "If you're working hard next to the goof-offs, management will notice sooner or later."

Tom turned to her, smiling warmly. He put a hand on her leg. "Thanks. I feel a little better."

She slid her hand down his back into his boxers, then moved it around to the front. And then she began . . . exploring.

"How much better?"

It was the next morning back at SOEL. Tom's floor was one huge room with dozens of cubicles in clusters lining narrow aisles. Most cubicles were occupied, but it was generally quiet, except for muted conversations and the low continuous clicking of keyboard strokes.

Tom was in his cubicle. Two adjacent monitors glowed with diagrams and data charts. Concentrating, he was shifting screen views constantly as he analyzed data and moved components around on the screens.

Tom heard audible sobbing coming from down the aisle and looked over his shoulder.

Ashley was walking by his cubicle. She was 26, with her lustrous red hair longer, and her green eyes brighter. She was a stunning young woman, but her eyes were irritated from crying.

Tom said quickly, "Hi."

Ashley stopped short, startled. "Oh! Hi!"

Tom stood at his chair and offered a hand to shake. "Tom Chandler. I started yesterday."

Ashley shook his hand while pinching the bridge of her nose and sniffling. Now she appeared to be embarrassed and felt a bit awkward. "Ashley Rogers. Good to meet you. Sorry I missed you yesterday."

Tom asked with concern, "Are you okay?"

Ashley looked away. "Oh, the 5-S Nazis got me."

Tom still hadn't learned about that. "I'm sorry, the what?"

She was not comfortable but offered, "I left in a hurry to get Jason at daycare . . . my son. He's six months."

Tom smiled, "That's sweet. I've got two, a girl and boy, five and two. Another one is on the way, in October."

Ashley cheered up a bit. "That's nice. Good for you."

Tom inquired directly, "So, the 5-S Nazis?"

"I was in such a hurry, I left a few folders with sensitive information out on my desk. When I got in today, I'd been hit with a citation."

Tom was rationally trying to understand. "What does a citation from the 5-S Nazis do to you?"

"It actually can count against your performance review, if you get a few. I guess you haven't had the training yet." But then she quickly said, "Hey, I have to get to work."

Tom nodded. "Oh, sure, sure, no problem."

Ashely said as she turned to walk on, "Let's meet downstairs for coffee or something. I want to hear about your kids."

"Absolutely, just let me know. Good to meet you."

Ashley smiled and continued to her cubicle, a few spaces down the row. Tom watched her until she was out of sight. He raised his eyebrows and gave a silent nod of approval, recalling that Pinocchio got a woody.

Chapter 6

THREE WEEKS LATER

The front door of the Chandler house opened and Tom walked in, carrying his briefcase, looking tired and dejected. He was immediately punched in the face by the overwhelming stench of human feces.

Deb called from the kitchen, "Hi Hun."

Tom called back, "Hey."

Looking around, he didn't see any signs of an obvious accident or mess. Walking into the living room, he couldn't see much except the boxes piled everywhere, each with an affixed moving company label. The small, flat screen television was on, blaring loud cheers and clapping from Wheel of Fortune. Since the sofa was covered with clothes and still more boxes, there was nowhere to sit.

Deb walked in from the kitchen and gave Tom a hug and a very quick peck. He lingered in a kissing posture, hoping for more. It didn't happen.

She said, "Mmm. Hi. I recorded Jeopardy for you. I didn't rewind the tape yet. We really need to get DVR. I'll call the cable company sometime."

"Okay, thanks," he said. "What in the world is that smell? Did septic back up or something?"

Deb rolled her eyes. "Nothing quite so dramatic. Kevin was in his room, had to go, but couldn't make it to the potty. He got his pants halfway down, but, umm, left his business in the hallway."

"Shit. On the rug?"

"No, at least it all happened on the wood floor. I cleaned it up a while ago. But get this. He didn't want to tell me, so he thought by covering the mess with a pile of his clothes, I wouldn't notice." She laughed. "Didn't come true."

Tom shook his head. "Poor guy. Maybe he should wear Pull-Ups for longer."

"I've got a load of his clothes going in the laundry, and the windows are all open upstairs."

"Thanks for taking care of that. At least he's getting better at the training."

"Are you hungry? I'll heat up your plate."

Tom passively muttered, "Sure. Thanks."

Deb noticed his mood, and joked, imitating Kramer, "How was your day today? Was it a good day today or a bad day today?"

He mumbled, "Wasted the whole day in sexual harassment training. Now I'm even more behind on the Cranston plans."

Deb tried to make light. "Teaching you how to harass?"

He was not particularly amused. "Very funny. Where are the kids now?"

"In the back. Emily caught a praying mantis in a jar and they've been catching other bugs to feed it. Flies, bees, ants."

"I guess that's a good nature lesson for them. Did you get any unpacking done?"

"Almost none. I've just been keeping up with the kids all day." Then she paused for a second. "We need to talk."

Tom's heart sank. That phrase never meant anything good, when any woman said that to any man. Ever. He knew it all too well, so he sighed. "I'll put my stuff away. Give me a few minutes, maybe we can talk while I eat."

Tom and Deb were sitting at the kitchen table as he ate the plate of microwaved leftovers. After shoving a large forkful of meatloaf into his mouth, he thought for a second. "At Foxwoods? What kind of work?"

"Serve at special events, like banquets and weddings. Mostly weekend afternoons and evenings."

Tom peered up at her and said with doubt, "While you're seven months pregnant?"

"I'll start in the fall, a few weeks after the baby."

He looked skeptical, and concerned.

Deb asked a bit defensively, "What?"

"I'll work fifty hours, then you'll waitress in a casino, while I watch the kids? And the baby? Evenings and weekends?"

"It's not like I'm a cocktail waitress at blackjack tables. It's just for special events. Just like I did in college."

Tom shook his head and took another bite. "That schedule sounds brutal, for both of us. Just thinking about it makes my eyebrows fall out."

"I don't know what that means. But I can dress sexy and flirt, and get big tips, especially from high-rollers. The pay is great for the hours. And the kids will never have to be in day care."

Tom thought, and then conceded some of those positive arguments. "Yeah, we will need the money. The real estate tax bill that just came was serious sticker shock. And we'll need a newer car before the baby gets here. The Windstar has just about had it."

"That extra income will help with the bills." She smiled and touched his arm, rubbing his skin lightly. "And I'll be able to get back in shape fast, after the baby."

As a result of her touch, he immediately felt a tingling, down there. "Speaking of that, when are we supposed to, you know, get quality alone time together? While we're working alternating shifts."

She smiled seductively. "By the time we do get together, we'll be really, really happy to see each other."

In a blandly furnished conference room at SOEL Headquarters, the walls, floor and furniture were as basic and conservative as they could be. Plenty of molded plastic and painted aluminum, and neutral shades or no color at all. Morton was standing in the front next to a projected image on the white board. Tom, Eric, Chuck, Ashley and several other engineers were sitting around the rectangular table. Each engineer had the same folder in front of them, opened to the first page.

Morton carped in a scolding tone, "Heretofore, this year, there have been so many 5-S infractions, our department has to take this refresher training."

Ashley shifted in her seat and flipped her hair behind her back.

Eric and Chuck had passive, uninterested expressions, until Eric leaned in and whispered, "Did he really just use the word 'heretofore?' What is this, regular London, on the real Thames River, four hundred years ago? Heretofore, I've never heard that word spoken in conversation in my whole life."

Tom's brow was wedged into an annoyed V as he folded his arms and sat back hard in his chair. Another f-ing wasted morning, he thought.

One hour later, Morton's forehead was beaded with sweat, and the armpits of his white shirt were stained and sopping wet. He was facing the slide on the white board, reading the projected bullets word for word.

His voice was a droning monotone, on and on and on. "The third S is Seiso, from the Japanese word that means shine. It can also be translated to mean scrub, sweep, or sanitize. We apply it to mean, clean and organize your workplace completely, and keep it clean. And all in the same process, we can use this cleaning as a mechanism for inspecting our workspace . . ."

Eric was staring ahead blankly, not listening. Chuck, his arms limp in his lap, was struggling to hold up heavy eyelids as his chin periodically dipped to his chest. Ashley had a small stack of specification sheets in her lap below table level and glanced down frequently to read them, accomplishing some productive work.

Tom, his face red and brow furrowed, raised his hand and said, "Jack?"

Morton stopped and turned to face them. "Tom, a question?"

"This presentation isn't worth the value of the air you're using to talk. Is there an online course we can take, or some other alternative?"

Morton said impatiently, "We all need to be here. Or we'll just have to take it again. Management and HR both require this."

Exasperated, Tom ran both hands through his hair and dropped them heavily to his thighs.

In a low growl he muttered, "Give me a pedicure with a belt sander while you're at it."

Chapter 7

THREE WEEKS LATER

The Southeast Connecticut Elementary School was a well-worn, one story, red brick building just off Route 12. The parking lot was buzzing with activity on this first day of the school year. Buses, cars and pedestrians constantly flowed back and forth over the fading asphalt.

The hallway inside the school was crowded with people moving in all directions. Scattered students were mostly escorted by parents or various school staff members. Deb was walking down the hall with Emily holding one hand, Kevin the other. They were working their way to the main office.

Suddenly, Kevin pulled her arm to a stop. Looking toward the floor, he yelped, "Mom!"

"What is it, sweetie?"

Emily burst out laughing, "He wet his pants!"

Kevin's shorts were sopping wet in the crotch and down the inside of both thighs. He was on the verge of tears, but yelled at Emily, "It's not funny!"

Deb quickly tried to mitigate the situation. "Oh, sweetie, I'm sorry. You were doing so well potty training at home lately. We should have put on a Pull-Up."

Kevin moaned, "I don't know where the potty is in school! I couldn't hold it!"

"That's okay. Let's drop off Emily and then we'll take care of it."

They continued walking with an increased sense of urgency. Kevin stepped gingerly with a bowlegged stride, like a strutting, chaps-wearing cowboy.

They soon arrived at the main office door.

Deb said to Emily, "You ready?"

"How will I know where to go?"

"I'm sure they'll tell us everything."

Kevin whined, "Where's the potty woom?"

The office administrative staff members were all frantically busy, answering questions posed by parents and students, and pointing them in the right directions. Emily and Kevin were standing on either side while Deb talked to one of the assistants.

She eyed Kevin's pants and said, "Does he need help?"

Deb quickly said, "We'll take care of that in a second. Where's the boys room?"

"Out the office to the left, on the right." The assistant flipped through the printed sheets of class rosters and said, "Chandler. Here she is. Emily has Ms. Flakus, room two. Just down the hall."

Deb asked, "Can I bring her down to her room?"

"That would be fine. I have all her forms. She's all set."

Deb quickly said to the assistant, "I want to talk to someone about volunteering. To be a class aid, on trips, and other activities. Whatever kinds of things parents can help with."

The assistant eyed her pregnant belly suspiciously and said, "Um, that would be great. We're always looking for active parents. It's a bit hectic today." She glanced at Kevin, who was uncomfortable and anxious. "Maybe you could check back next week?"

Deb said quickly, "Sure. Be glad to." Then she said to Emily, "Ready to see your room? Kevin, we'll take care of you in a second."

After dropping off Emily at her class, Deb and Kevin were in the boys restroom. Kevin's pants were completely off, and Deb had wrapped his sopping wet briefs in paper towels. She dabbed his shorts quickly with more paper towels and told him, "You'll have to put these back on. You can't walk through the school without pants on."

Kevin tentatively pulled up his shorts but quickly squealed, "They're still wet!"

"I know. But you'll have to wear them like that until we get home. It's just for a few more minutes." She thought for a second. "While we're walking, and in the car, try waving your hand back and forth in front of your pants, like this." She demonstrated in front of herself. "The wind from moving your hand might help them dry faster."

Kevin attempted as she had shown, waving his hand back and forth in front of his pants. After a few seconds, realizing his shorts were just as wet, he looked up and cried in distress, "It's not working!"

Deb managed to smile. "Okay, okay, just keep trying and let's get home."

THREE WEEKS LATER

In the basement of the Chandler house, a repairman, heavy, scruffy, and dressed in dirty blue work clothes, was kneeling on the floor. As he closed his tool box, four inches of butt crack extended above his belt.

Emily and Kevin were giggling, standing just outside the utility room.

The repairman stood as he wiped his hands with a dirty rag. He stood next to the furnace near Tom, and Deb, who was more than eight months pregnant.

Tom asked the repairman, "What's the diagnosis?"

He said in gruff voice, "If you go the winter with this unit like it is, at best it's gonna break down. You won't have heat, and your pipes will probably freeze and burst. That's the good news. The bad news is, at the worst, your house will burn down."

Tom instantly felt a wave of nausea. "What? Seriously?"

"You think I'm going for laughs here? It's the original furnace in this house. I worked on it before you guys moved in. When was this house built, anyway?"

Tom thought a second. "About twenty-five years ago."

"Twenty-five New England winters. This one lasted pretty good. You should get a new one before it gets cold out."

Tom hesitated, then asked, while holding his breath, "How much would that cost?"

He calculated in his head. "A good one, for this size house? About eighty-two, installed."

Tom gasped, "Eight-two hundred?"

"Capacity and connected for baseboard in three zones. Good for thirty years if you keep it clean and use our high grade oil."

Deb quickly piped in, "We'll just have to figure out a way to pay for it."

Tom turned on her, and raised his voice sharply, "Figure out a way? What, put more Miracle Grow on our money tree?"

Deb said, louder still, "Or what? Have no heat? Or a fire hazard? With the kids in the house, and the baby?"

Emily appeared behind them and said with concern, "Why are you guys yelling?"

Deb said to her, "It's okay, sweetie, we're just trying to figure this out." To the repairman, Deb said politely, "Thanks so much. We'll call in a couple days."

The Repairman shrugged and picked up his toolbox. "Might take two weeks for a unit to ship. We can make the work order an emergency so it gets done faster. I'll mail you today's invoice."

Tom grumbled, "Bury me up to my neck in Death Valley without sunblock."

A while later, Deb was sitting on the edge of their bed on the comforter. Partially unpacked boxes were still cluttered in uneven piles against two walls. The room door was closed and Tom was pacing slightly, his arms animated, emphasizing his words.

Tom asked firmly, "How?"

"The credit union does personal loans for this kind of thing. I heard they approve them quickly, and the interest isn't too bad."

Irritated, he said, "I know we can get a loan! We can always get a loan! Or use a credit card! How do we make the payments? On top of the car payment?"

"You want us all at risk for a fire? I wouldn't be able to sleep!"

Tom paced, and ran a hand through his hair. "And they're cutting back overtime. No more than ten hours a week until new contracts come through."

Deb offered, "I'll start working soon."

Tom thought for a second. "Maybe we should get another price quote. What's the oil company in town? Andersen? They do . . ."

Deb yelled, exasperated, "The furnace is twenty-five years old! It needs to be replaced! We knew it wouldn't last long when we bought the house!"

But as she finished emotionally explaining, she suddenly clutched her belly, grimacing. "Ow. Ooo!"

Tom stopped pacing and said with concern, "What? Are you okay?"

Deb shifted back and forth, holding her belly, grimacing. "Ow. That's not right. Ow! Ow!"

She shifted positions again, and then her expression changed from discomfort to surprise. She placed a hand under her shorts for a few seconds, then pulled it out. Her hand was glistening wet.

Tom gasped in a high voice, "Your water?"

She said sarcastically, "Well, that changes our short-term priorities."

Tom quickly became more focused. "Better pack a bag, or something. I'll call the sitter."

Deb stood gingerly and looked down at the bed. "I've ruined the comforter."

EIGHTEEN MINUTES LATER

Their slightly used blue Volvo wagon was driving too fast north on Route 12, a two lane state road along the Thames River, through the Connecticut countryside. The foliage on the maples and birches was just beginning to change, but Tom and Deb didn't come close to noticing.

As Tom drove, he glanced continuously back and forth at Deb, who was sitting uncomfortably in the passenger's seat on a towel.

She said, "Good thing we got a car with leather seats."

Tom said helplessly, "Cross your legs."

Deb muttered in a strained whisper, "That sounds like sound, professional medical advice. Stuff is happening pretty fast."

"Contractions? We're only ten minutes away. Hang on, just hang on."

Deb grimaced and said, "Hang on? To what?"

Chapter 8

Less than half an hour later, Tom and Deb were in the delivery room at the hospital. Leaning against the raised back of the bed, Deb's hair was wet and matted, and her red, strained face was drenched and glistening with sweat. Tom, dressed in blue hospital scrubs, was behind the bed near her head, trying to give moral support.

The doctor, a middle-aged woman, mostly concealed in her mask, cap and gown, cried with encouragement, "That's it! One more huge push! One more!"

Tom was tense, feeling useless, but said supportively, "Come on, Babe. One more push!"

Deb was gasping, straining, her face beet red. "Oh GOD!"

She let out one more strained, prolonged shriek, "Uhh!" lasting several seconds. The sound filled the room and could be heard down the hallway.

Then she exhaled completely, all air passing from her lungs, and her entire body relaxed, almost to the point of collapse.

The doctor cried, "Here . . . she comes! It's a girl!"

Deb laid back with a spent smile, her eyes closing. "Oh God."

Tom yelped in relief, "A girl! A baby sister!" He looked up at the doctor. "Does she have all her parts?"

The doctor was working on the baby, wiping her down. As she aspirated her nostrils and mouth with a light suction hose, there were muffled slurping sounds. Soon, very soft, broken crying began.

The doctor said quietly, "She's perfectly healthy."

Tom whispered to Deb, "Holy shit. Little Kaitlyn?"

Deb forced an exhausted smile and nodded. "Kaitlyn Marie."

Tom said softly, "You did it, Babe. You made a brand new Chandler."

Tom reached for her hand, tangled up in an IV tube, but they held hands anyway. The doctor had finished cleaning and loosely wrapping Kaitlyn in light linen. She handed her to Deb, who anxiously took her and cradled her close.

Tom's smile was ear to ear under his mask and silent tears rolled down his cheeks. He lightly touched Kaitlyn's head and felt a warmth he had forgotten he could feel.

The next morning, Tom brought Kevin and Emily to Deb's room to meet their new baby sister. When they quietly walked into the room, Deb was holding Kaitlyn in a first attempt to nurse. She draped the small hospital blanket over herself and shifted positions.

"Hi kids," she smiled, when they got closer to the bed.

"Hi hun," said Tom sweetly. "Did the night go okay?"

"Sure," she said. "Mostly she was in the nursery but they brought her in once for contact. I even slept a little."

Emily and Kevin were standing back a bit, unsure of how close they were allowed to come. Deb saw that, and decided it would be better to nurse later. Under the blanket, she quickly closed up her gown and held Kaitlyn a bit away from herself. "Would you guys like to meet your little sister?"

Emily and Kevin walked tentatively to the bedside. Tom saw that Kevin couldn't really see over the side so he lifted him up to sit on the edge of the bed.

Kevin studied Kaitlyn curiously for a few seconds, lying quietly in Deb's arms, then asked, "Is it real?"

Deb smiled widely. "This isn't a doll, it's your brand new baby sister."

Emily asked sincerely, "Can I name her?"

Tom was going to remind her she already had a name, but instead asked, "What name were you thinking of?"

"I really want to name her Precious Cupcake. It's so pretty."

Deb tried not to laugh out loud and managed to say, "That is a very pretty name. But Daddy and I already gave her a name. This is Kaitlyn, Kaitlyn Marie. Maybe we'll call her Kaity."

Kevin's nose crinkled up. Emily was going to protest, but instead asked, "Can I hold her?"

Deb said, "Sure, you can each take a turn, but we need to be very gentle with her. Em, climb up and sit here next to me."

Tom helped situate Emily so Deb could secure Kaitlyn gently in her arms.

The five members of the Chandler family all quietly visited and took turns tenderly holding baby Kaitlyn.

SIX WEEKS LATER

In the living room, Tom was sitting on the sofa holding Kaitlyn in one hand, a small bottle of expelled breast milk in the other. The low volume on the television announced a football game, creating a white noise murmur in the room. Tom occasionally glanced up at the game, then back to feeding Kaitlyn.

Fast footfalls of little feet ran down the hardwood stairs, down the hall, and to the living room. Emily burst in, followed quickly by Kevin. And then slower, hard-heeled footfalls could be heard coming down the stairs.

Emily said with excitement, "Daddy! You should see Mommy!"

Followed by Kevin, "She looks like she's getting married!"

Kaitlyn fussed slightly. Tom adjusted his hold on her, and propped the bottle up a bit more vertical. He said to the kids, "Mommy's going to her new job."

Emily's face scrunched up. "She looks funny. She doesn't look like our mommy."

Tom said quietly, "Be nice, please."

Deb walked into the living room. She was wearing a frilled teal blouse emblazoned with a logo, and a short black skirt. Black stockings and thick-healed black shoes completed the ensemble. Her hair was tied back tightly, and she was wearing more make-up than usual.

She spread her arms for a full view, then placed her hands on her hips and struck a pseudo-sexy modeling pose. "What do you think?"

Tom gave her a sad smile. "I'm not sure that's the look that works best for you."

Deb said, "As if. I make this look hot. Admit it."

"You're always hot. Especially for a mother of . . . three," he said.

"You got that right."

He just smiled. "What's the gig tonight?"

"Baseball legends banquet. Some famous players will be there. To benefit First Responders."

"People buy tickets to have dinner with famous players?"

"Something like that. Most people there will probably be tribal executives, and high-rollers. I think the players are mostly older Red Sox and Yankees. If I can get them, do you want any autographs?"

Tom shrugged, and Kaitlyn fussed again. "Sure, that sounds fun. Anyone on the Red Sox would be great. If Dewey Evans or Jim Rice are there, but I guess that's too much to hope for. I remember them when I was a little kid."

"I'll see what the process is, and do what I'm allowed." She turned to Kevin and Emily, who were still looking at her like she was wearing a Halloween costume. "Did you guys take your baths?"

Kevin yelped, "No bath!"

Tom said, "When Kait goes down, I'll get them going on that."

Deb looked at the television. "Is this the Patriots?"

"No, they won earlier. It was an incredible comeback. Brady is still pretty amazing. I may have to become a real fan again. This is the later game. The Broncos are plastering the Jets."

"Okay, well, I'd better get going." To the kids she added, "You guys be good for Dad. See you in the morning." She gathered up her purse and keys, and slipped on a light jacket.

Emily said to Tom, "Can I feed her the rest of the bottle?"

Tom said, "Sure. Here, sit here."

Emily climbed to the center of the sofa as Tom stood. He then gently situated Kaitlyn on Emily's lap, placed the bottle so Kaitlyn could feed, and so Emily could hold it upright.

Kevin felt left out and asked, "Can I he'p?"

"You have a very important job. Sit right here and keep Kait's head up." He helped Kevin climb up and slide to the right spot, and had him gently support Kaitlyn's head with both hands. "That's perfect. You're both doing a great job."

Deb was watching them, and suddenly became very sad. Tom soon caught her expression and walked over.

He said quietly to her, "The start of our new schedule, our new lifestyle."

She was becoming teary-eyed. "I'm going to miss so much of their lives, day in and day out."

"I guess we both will, just at different times of the day. And I guess we'll miss a lot of each other, too."

She shook her head, "Tag team parents. What an f-ing concept."

He tried to sound optimistic. "No day-care, at least, and not much baby-sitting until they're older."

She said, almost to herself, "I wonder what the heck this will do to our marriage."

Tom shrugged. "We'll either be madly in love, or we'll kill each other."

"That sure narrows it down." Deb gave one last look as Emily and Kevin fed infant Kaitlyn. "I guess I'd better get going."

Tom and Deb kissed quickly and she headed out the front door.

Kaitlyn was finally asleep in her crib. The same crib Emily had slept in until she was almost three, and Kevin had slept in until six weeks prior.

Emily and Kevin were playing with toys together in the bathtub as Tom settled in to wash them. They were splashing and laughing loudly, throwing toys back and forth, dumping cups of water on each other's heads. From the warm water and the active fun in the tub, their hair was wet and cheeks were flushed.

Tom reminded them, "We'll have to keep the noise down, please. Kaity's asleep."

"Mommy lets us splash," complained Emily.

"I know, but it's only me now. If Kaity wakes up, I won't be able to help her until you're in your jammies."

Kevin slapped his hands loudly on the water several times, continuing to laugh. In spite of his earlier protests, he was having a jolly time. Tom was busy pulling together wash clothes and children's body wash and didn't bother to repeat his request for quiet.

Emily suddenly said, "Look! Kevin's dinky is straight!"

Tom took note of that comment and looked down. In fact, as she correctly pointed out, Kevin's little penis was erect.

Tom said, a bit awkwardly, "That's okay, probably the warm water and playing feel good to him. I'd better get you guys washed and out."

Tom initiated a small assembly line, washing and rinsing Emily, and coaxing her to dry off and put on her own pajamas in her room. He then washed and rinsed Kevin, got him dried and wrapped in a towel, and went with him, scurrying to his room for his pajamas.

While Tom read them both their favorite children's book, Amy and the Orca, about a little girl who befriends an orca whale pod with her flute playing, Kaitlyn remained quiet in her crib. After a bit of negotiating and complaining, the kids finally settled quietly into bed for the night.

After Tom checked on Kaitlyn, who was content and asleep, he settled downstairs in the living room. He was alone in a quiet house for the first time in a long time.

He sat on the sofa, not quite sure what he should be doing. But he knew he was tired. He turned on the television and flipped through channels until he found an old movie that he found interesting.

After twenty minutes, he fell asleep where he sat, his head nodding back, his mouth hanging open.

Their new life had begun. Split shifts of work, split shifts of child care, for the foreseeable future.

Without ceremony or fanfare, or any idea where they would be physically and emotionally ten and a half years in the future.

Chapter 9

TEN AND A HALF YEARS LATER

Present Day

Deb was at the kitchen table busily writing on a yellow legal pad, with fourteen-inch-long sheets of paper. Tom walked in and she quickly stopped writing, pulled the pad closer, and covered it with her left arm. He glanced at her with amusement, and shook his head. Continuing to the refrigerator, he pulled out a bottle of water.

As he was leaving the kitchen he said, "I don't think our lists are supposed to be kept secret from each other."

She simply said, "Asshole."

"Ah, so sweet. Well, I'd better get cracking on mine. There is so very much to write."

Deb quickly snapped, "That's why I'm using a legal pad. There's much more room for my extensive list of grievances."

A rather fancy restaurant occupied a very rustic colonial house just outside downtown Mystic. Formal dining was on the main floors of the house but there was a small, casual pub in the basement. Beautiful field stones and stained hardwood made up most of the furnishings in that fairly small room.

There was one empty wooden table sitting close to the field stone fireplace along one wall. A roaring wood fire crackled loudly, spitting sparks and flames high into the chimney. The darkened room was quaint and romantic.

A waitress walked over and laid two menus on the table. Deb and Tom followed her and sat down, almost reluctantly.

The waitress waited until they were settled and said, "I'll be back in a second to take your drink order." She pointed to a slate panel with hand-written selections. "Local brew specials are on the board. We just got a great imperial stout from Tox Brewing. They call it, Black Widow."

Deb asked her, "Tox Brewing? What's that?"

The waitress explained, "The fairly new craft brewery in New London. All their beers are named for toxic plants and animals. Black widow, deadly nightshade, fire coral. But they all taste great!"

Deb smiled faintly and said, "That sounds great. Thanks."

The waitress left and went about her work.

Deb sat silently, checking out the room and the other patrons, scattered at a few tables and at the bar. "It's actually kind of cool in here. What a waste of a perfectly nice pub that we're here for this 'big date.'"

Tom glanced over at the specials board briefly and said nothing.

Deb said, "Toxic Brew. That sounds exactly like what we need."

Tom suddenly pulled a folded white paper from his shirt pocket. "If we're really going to do this . . ."

She reached into her purse. "We are. This was your super bright idea."

"Let's try to do this systematically and productively. At least try to find positive things to build on."

"What . . . ever. I couldn't think of too many good things, to tell you the truth. Not sure what we'll build on."

Tom unfolded his paper on the table. Deb spread out her long yellow sheet. Words were not legible to each other, but on both sheets, the listed items on one side were much more extensive than on the other.

Tom leaned over and pointed to her longer list. "Are those your bad things?"

She nodded, and pointed to his long list. "Those are yours?"

Tom nodded. "Shit," he muttered.

"What's the top thing on your bad list?"

Tom picked up his sheet. "We almost never have sex, and when we do, it's mechanical and cold. Like a chore, or something to just get out of the way. It used to be so good." He shook his head. "What's your top bad thing?"

"I never do anything but work. And take care of the house, and run errands. Not having good sex is about eighth on my list."

Tom scanned his list. "Only work and take care of the house and yard is third on my list. Crushing and oppressive debt is second."

She said, "I don't have that on mine. I forgot to write that down. I guess it should be near the top. What's top on your 'good' list?"

Tom didn't have to look at his sheet. "Emily, Kevin and Kaitlyn."

Deb looked away. "Mine too."

"I like our house. And this is a nice area to live."

She shrugged.

For a couple minutes, they both sat in stunned silence, staring at nothing.

Tom said, "Okay, so I guess we keep the kids, and we don't move."

Deb was quiet for a while, and finally said, "We need help."

He said, without sarcasm, "We finally agree on something. I don't know what, but we definitely need something."

They sat quietly for a couple more minutes while thoughts raced through their minds. Finally, the waitress walked over.

She was pathologically cheerful and asked, "What drinks can I get to start you off?"

Tom and Deb looked at each other and then stared at her for a second.

Deb finally asked, "Just how toxic is that imperial stout? What did you say it was called? Black widow?"

The waitress smiled widely, thought a second, and said without humor, "Yes, Black Widow. Alcohol by volume, 8.5%."

Tom said, "Perfect. Bring two of those. As quickly as possible."

Chapter 10

The kitchen was bustling with activity as Kevin and Kaitlyn ate at the table. Tom had an assembly line of sandwich-making in full production on the counter. When the sandwiches were made he stuffed them in vinyl lunch bags. He then added an assortment of other random prepared foods, attempting to imitate the trappings of a square meal in each sack.

Emily yelled loudly, before she even arrived in the kitchen, "Dad! That brat buttered my phone again!"

Tom abruptly stopped working on the lunches and looked at Kevin. "You have got to be kidding me!"

Emily, now 15, trim and pretty with long brown hair, stormed into the kitchen, brandishing her iPhone. "Look at this!"

She made dagger eyes at Kevin as she held the phone so Tom could look closer. Butter was smeared all over its screen.

Kevin exclaimed, "She's always on that stupid phone!" He had a wry, satisfied grin until Tom stepped closer and bent over so their noses were a foot apart.

Tom growled angrily, "If you ever do that again, you will buy her a new phone. Even if you have to pay for it out of your allowance for five years."

Suddenly sheepish, Kevin said, "Okay. Sorry."

Emily carefully used a damp dish rag to wash her phone in the kitchen sink. She inspected it, then announced loudly, "I'm going."

Tom was surprised, looking up at the clock. "Is the bus this early?"

Emily said, "Doug's driving me."

That didn't clarify anything for Tom. "Who's Doug?"

"Dad, where have you been? We've been friends for three weeks."

Kevin said, without looking up. "When you're fishing without bait, sometimes you get lucky and just snag something on the empty hook."

Tom yelled, "Kevin!" He then turned back to Emily. "You have a friend that drives?"

Emily rolled her eyes, "Uh, yeah. He's a junior."

Tom was stunned. "Can he come in for a second?"

"Not now! We're late! See you later!"

Emily hurried out of the kitchen, grabbing her backpack. Tom started to say something but stopped as she was already gone. The front door slammed behind her.

Tom turned back to finish making lunches. He asked Kevin and Kaitlyn directly, "Do you guys know this Doug?"

Kaitlyn piped up, "Of course. He's so cute!"

Tom looked very concerned, but didn't ask anything else about him. "Are you both almost done? I'll drop you off on my way to work."

Kevin said, "Mom always takes us."

"She got home really late last night. I'll do it today. She'll pick you up at school later."

A wide-bodied shuttle bus was sitting motionless at a traffic light, stuck in bumper-to-bumper traffic. The light changed to green, then red, seemingly much too quickly. All vehicles moved forward only two car lengths.

Tom was sitting in a seat next to a window, looking at the time on his iPhone, straining ahead to assess traffic. He shook his head and swore silently.

But then he reconsidered. Why should I be worried? Maybe it just doesn't matter anymore.

That evening, Tom and Deb were sitting on the sofa in the living room. The television flashed a Red Sox game, but the sound was muted. Half empty glasses of wine were on the coffee table.

Tom said, "Ashley didn't care, she has kids of her own. She gets it. But I was late for the department meeting."

Deb muttered, "What am I supposed to do? I got home at three!"

"I know, I know! Don't even start with that. I don't think it matters at work anymore. I'm just . . . you know," he emphasized with a sarcastic whine and a back and forth hand motion, "communicating!"

Deb snapped, "Add that to your list, why don't you."

Tom lashed out with, "Why don't you just tap hydrochloric acid into my shower!" He quickly swallowed the rest of his wine in one gulp. He sat quietly fuming, slowly turning the empty glass in his hand. Finally he said, "We're never going to be able to really talk anything through. Not with the shit-storms all around us every day."

"Why even bother. Things at your work don't matter. Do things at home even matter?"

He glared at her. "You want to call it quits? Is that what you're saying?"

Deb looked away and shook her head. She bit her lower lip, starting to tear up. "No, I don't. I don't know. I'm just so exhausted. There's nothing to look forward to, nothing fun."

He spit out a laugh, "Yeah, with me too."

Deb went sarcastic with, "If we could just slip away to talk. Maybe a month in a stilted hut, in Bora Bora."

"We could only afford three weeks." He thought a second and then said seriously, "How about a long weekend somewhere?"

She rolled her eyes. "We'll probably end up killing each other if we're ever alone for more than a few minutes."

Tom seriously asked, "When's your next weekend off?"

She thought, remembering, "Two weeks. Nothing after Wednesday that week."

"Just to stop the noise so we can talk through some of this. Some place not too far, that we can drive to. Cape Cod, Vermont, something like that."

"Just sounds like more debt to me."

"A couple hundred bucks won't make any difference. Hotels are cheaper this time of year."

Deb was not convinced but said, without enthusiasm, "I guess so."

Tom analyzed things in his head for a second. "Emily is old enough to babysit. I'll see what I can find on line."

She finished her wine. "Banner idea."

TWO WEEKS LATER

Two small matching suitcases were standing in the living room towards the front door. Emily, Kevin and Kaitlyn were on the sofa and Tom and Deb were standing in front of them.

Kaitlyn complained, "I want to come."

Deb explained, "No, honey, Mom and Dad are going away for the weekend. Just the two of us."

Kevin stated accurately, "You've never done that before, without us."

Kaitlyn asked, "Where are you going?"

"The coast of Maine, to a bed and breakfast," said Deb. "It's a house that's like a small hotel. We just want to take it easy for a couple days."

Kevin asked with genuine concern, "How will we get supper?"

Tom said, "Emily will take care of everything. How about pizza tonight, and Chinese food tomorrow? Both those restaurants can deliver. There's plenty of milk and cereal, and peanut butter and jelly and bread, for sandwiches."

Kaitlyn asked with expectation, "Chuck E. Cheese?"

"The one near us closed," Tom said. "And I think they've filed for bankruptcy. Em will figure it out. Maybe Fireside Pizza."

"We'll be back Sunday," said Deb. "No friends over. It's okay if you watch a lot of TV."

"We can do it, Mom," Emily said seriously.

Deb smiled, "I know you can. We'll call a couple times to see how it's going."

Tom said very deliberately, "Kevin, no magnifying glass art. Em, no visits from Doug."

Emily rolled her eyes. "Get real. I know."

Chapter 11

The bed and breakfast was a quaint, lovely inn built in the 1800s. Tom and Deb parked the Volvo wagon under coach lights, nestled among evergreen trees in front of a rustic, detached barn. They climbed to the porch under antique lamps, checked in at reception, and made their way up the central staircase.

The wooden, white door swung open and Tom entered their room pulling his suitcase, with Deb immediately behind. They paused and scanned the furnishings.

Tom said, "This isn't bad. It's kind of cozy."

Deb didn't comment but instead asked, "Who's Trudy?"

"What?"

"On the door," she said, "there's a sign that says this is 'Trudy's Room.'"

Tom remembered something from the online booking. "I think she was the original owner's daughter, or something like that."

Deb walked further into the room. "Gertrude. Now there's a name we forgot to consider for our girls. That, and Precious Cupcake are clear oversights on our part."

Tom rolled his suitcase to the wall and threw his jacket on the bed. He looked around briefly. "Where's the bathroom?"

"Across the hall. When we checked in the hostess said it's not in the room."

He said with annoyance, "A hundred and fifty bucks a night, and we have to cross the hall to take a piss?"

Deb was even more annoyed with his tone. "Would you at least try to enjoy this?"

"Our own house is more convenient. The toilet is eight steps from our bed."

Deb raised her voice. "We should've just stayed home then, and locked ourselves in our room!"

Sarcastically, he added, "Then we could've used this money to pay off all our debt. All of it, and then retire to that stilted hut in Bora Bora."

Deb roughly pushed down her suitcase and flopped heavily into a chair. "Damn it!"

He turned around, walked across the room, and looked out a window. "This weekend is going to be a real hootenanny. Just like the last time I picked shards of broken glass out of my eyeballs."

Still in the room two hours later, Deb was on her iPhone, sitting in a chair by the window. Tom was sitting in bed, holding a science fiction novel titled <u>Convergent</u>, listening to her instead of reading.

She listened for a while longer, then, "No, no, don't flush it again! Take the cover off the tank . . . okay. See the metal rod with the black ball? Lift that until you hear the water stop running."

Tom said absently, "It needs new tank hardware."

Covering the phone, she snapped at him, "Would you knock it off!" Into the phone, she said, "Okay, see the black round plug at the bottom? Just tap that until it falls and seals the hole in the tank. Good, perfect, now let go of the ball and the water should start filling the tank."

Five minutes later, Deb was still on the phone. "He did what? Ant dances? What are ant dances?" She listened for a minute. "Uh huh, okay, I see. Please ask him never to do that again. We'll talk to him when we get home. Thanks for taking care of it all. Love you."

Deb pressed the hang up button and put down her phone. "Em thinks it had been running for hours before she noticed."

"We're lucky it wasn't flooding the whole upstairs."

Deb shook her head at him. "You're such a big help."

"What am I supposed to do, two hundred miles away?"

"How about not complaining about something while it's happening! And why didn't you explain how to stop a running toilet?"

"She called you. I'm afraid to ask, but what are ant dances?"

Deb explained dryly, "Your son found some big black ants in the basement. He put a couple in a pot on the stove, turned on the heat, and watched them start to dance. And then they danced faster. And then they did a very fast jitterbug. Until they couldn't dance anymore, with a hiss and puff of smoke."

Tom's mouth dropped open. "Jesus, that is just lovely. Who would think to do something like that?"

Deb said quickly, "Our son would. I mean, your son."

"I really have to talk to him." Tom was thinking about what else that implied. "And, the better news is, we have carpenter ants."

Deb got up and moved to open her suitcase. "I'm getting ready for bed."

Tom said sarcastically, "Is this a bad time to talk about money problems?"

She gave him a dirty look, dug into her suitcase and pulled out a toiletry bag and night gown. She yanked open the room door and slammed it behind her as she mumbled, "You really are an ass."

Tom said, "Thank you. And make sure you don't prance naked across the hallway, coming back from our very convenient bathroom."

Chapter 12

The otherwise picturesque village of Freeport, Maine was fairly crowded with cars and people moving in all directions. On that early spring afternoon, the sun was high and the temperature was comfortable.

Tom and Deb were strolling slowly down the sidewalk, blankly glancing at store fronts, signs and pedestrians that passed by. They were passively glum, not talking, not looking at each other. There was a bustle of conversation and noise all around, but not from them.

Tom finally asked, rhetorically, "Do you want to go anywhere in particular?"

"Not really, I don't know. It is cute here, though. Pretty town."

Tom nodded to his right, "There's LL Bean. They have good stuff. Didn't you say you need jeans?"

"Aren't they expensive?"

He shrugged, "Kind of, but high quality." Then he saw another sign a little further up. "The clearance outlet is around the corner, down the hill. The stuff in there should all be discounted."

Deb perked up a bit, now with a plan. "Good idea. Let's go there and see what they've got."

The aisles of the clearance outlet were narrow and packed with racks of shirts, pants, jackets and shoes. And it was crowded. People moved around displays and each other, back and forth, as they searched through the many stacks and shelves.

Deb was flipping through a jacket rack, holding several pairs of jeans flung over her arm. Tom walked to her cradling a few shirts.

He said, "Do you see anything you like?"

She held up her jeans, "These look good. I need to try them on. Maybe one of these jackets, too."

He nodded, "Yeah, me too. These shirts are nice, and the prices are really reduced. I could wear these to work."

Deb noticed one of the shirts he held was monogramed with cursive initials, stitched into one cuff. She pulled up the sleeve and read, "LMZ?" while looking up at him. "You're going to wear this to work? Are you changing your name so your initials will match?"

Tom shrugged, "It's a seventy-five dollar shirt reduced to ten dollars. It was probably never picked up by LMZ. I usually roll up the sleeves on shirts like this anyway."

She just narrowed her eyes and inspected more jackets that she could try on.

Outside the entrance to the dressing rooms, several people were in line holding items for fitting, women to the right, men to the left. Tom and Deb were waiting separately, now at the front of each line. They watched as a woman left one of the rooms and headed for checkout.

Tom waved his hand and said to Deb, "That's you. I'll get the next men's room."

Deb had become impatient waiting and said, "Just come in with me. We can do this together and save everyone time. And my blood sugar is getting low. I need to eat dinner soon."

Tom was visibly hesitant. "Those are the women's rooms."

Deb laughed with annoyance. "Oh, come off it. No one is going to care."

Tom looked around as if he was about to commit a crime, then followed Deb to the empty dressing room.

After they entered, he closed and latched the wood, slotted door. It looked more like an undersized window shutter than a door, and didn't reach the floor. It would be easy for anyone to look through the slots if they had wanted to do so.

Deb tossed the jeans on the bench and started to unbutton her pants. Tom hung up his shirts on a wall hook. He started to unbutton his shirt but stopped as he caught sight of Deb. Inadvertently, he stood there gawking at her.

She slid down and removed her pants, revealing lacy, pink panties. Her face was expressionless as she unfolded a new pair of jeans, checking the labels. That is, until she caught sight of Tom staring at her below the waist, at her panties.

She stopped what she was doing and asked, "What?"

Tom was embarrassed that he was caught ogling, but said, "Are those panties new? They're kind of sexy."

Deb rolled her eyes. "Yeah, I got them for this weekend, if, you know. If we started getting along better." She watched him staring at her. "It's been a long time since you looked at me that way. Do YOU see anything you like?"

Tom looked away and said, "You look good. You are in really good shape."

Deb said, "I am on my feet for thirty hours a week." But then said, very sincerely, "Thanks. That's sweet of you."

Tom smiled faintly and took off his shirt, tossing it aside.

Deb gave him an appraising scan up and down. She said, "You look good too. I do like your hairy chest."

"Thanks," he smiled.

Deb sized him up a bit longer, then dropped the jeans she was holding. She stepped closer to him, put both hands on his chest, and started caressing the hair there.

Tom whispered urgently, "What in the world are you doing?"

She said, in a gravelly, sultry voice, "Trying to get along better."

She leaned in and kissed him on the side of his neck, then his chin, then on his mouth. She held the last kiss while she moved a hand from his chest to unbuckle his belt. Tom was startled and jumped back, almost leaving his feet while nearly losing his balance.

He whispered frantically, "What are you doing?"

She smiled seductively, "I am pretty sure my leprosy is in remission, too."

Tom urgently rasped, "We'll get arrested!"

"Maybe. But I'll bet you dinner tonight that you won't stop me."

Tom's expression was dread and horror as Deb bent to her knees, kissing him continuously as she moved lower, then lower still. He looked down, then nervously towards the door, then back down at her. His belt buckle clacked open and his jeans fell with a swish to the floor. Tom closed his eyes and tilted back his head, with his mouth hanging open. He was gasping for breath.

He suddenly opened his eyes and watched Deb stand up and move back a couple steps. His mouth was still hanging open as he looked nervously back and forth toward the door several times. Then his eyes moved up, then down, then up again, and suddenly Deb's pink panties flew at him and landed on his head. He quickly pulled them off and flung them aside to the bench.

He said quietly, frantically, "Holy shit. What . . .?"

Deb said, very seductively, "You'll have to be quick, and very, very quiet."

Tom stood wide-eyed, looked at the door, then moved toward her.

Several impatient customers were waiting in line outside the dressing rooms. The noises in the store permeated the air and drown out sounds that may, or may not have been coming from the dressing rooms.

An elderly man looked at his watch and shook his head. He was clearly very annoyed. He turned to the customer in line behind him and complained about how long some people took just to try on some clothes.

Seven Minutes Later

The gazes of all the people waiting in line shifted in unison toward one of the women's dressing room doors that opened suddenly. Tom and Deb hurried out, one behind the other, across the customer lines and into the main floor space of the store. Deb was straightening her jacket and flipping back her hair. Tom was conspicuously holding his shirts directly in front of his crotch, trying not to reveal that his jeans were, at the moment, much too tight.

The same elderly man eyed them suspiciously as they passed, and complained, "A lot of people are waiting, you know!"

Without comment, and without making eye contact, they tossed the clothes, that were never tried on, over an end display and quickly headed for the exit.

Chapter 13

Tom and Deb burst through the door of their room at the bed and breakfast, laughing hysterically. They fell together on the bed, flushed and gasping for breath.

Tom cried, "I can't believe we just did that! What was up with you?"

Deb shrugged and grinned, "Caught up in the moment, I guess. And trying to . . . get along better?" Just for that moment, they gazed at each other, smiling.

"That old guy in line was mad at us. I think he heard something!"

Deb said dismissively, "Oh, who cares. If he did, he'll just have a funny story to tell."

"He sure wasn't laughing. I guess we'll have a story to tell, too."

Deb laughed, "A pretty short story. That was no Tolstoy novel. Five minutes, if even." She suddenly noticed that her pants didn't feel quite right, and rubbed her hand along the front of her thigh. "Whoops. I left those sexy panties in the dressing room. Evidence left at the scene of the crime."

"Aw, too bad. Those were nice. I guess we can't go back and get them."

She laughed. "I don't think we can ever go to LL Bean again. Police should be knocking on this room door any minute now."

"It's been a while since we did reverse cowgirl."

"And the first time in a long time in a public place, probably since our honeymoon. Well, that was a hiking trail in New Hampshire. That isn't really public. Not in a bed or a car, anyway."

Tom sat up. "Think to come of it, that makes, what, three New England states? Connecticut, New Hampshire, and now Maine."

She laughed, but said only half joking, "We should try for all six."

"Yeah, right." He analyzed that possibility for a second. "Rhode Island? We only live 20 minutes from the border. Get a hotel room just to, 'check that box?'" He accented the last statement with air quotes.

"Or maybe a public place in every New England state, like we just did. Like a Watch Hill beach in Rhode Island, or somewhere like that."

Tom shook his head, saying, "I don't know about that. That was a little too exciting for me."

"Oh, come on. You're such a prude."

Tom compromised with, "On the hiking trail was kind of fun, out in nature. I could do something like that again."

"The highest point of elevation in each New England state. How about that? They're probably all on hiking trails."

"You mean, hike to the highest points in each New England state, just to 'do it' at the top of each one?"

Deb shrugged, "Sounds like an adventurous challenge."

"And the kids, while all this . . . adventure . . . is going on?"

"I don't know. We'll have to figure it out each trip. Emily's old enough to babysit, like she is now, even as we speak."

Tom considered the challenge. "Maybe I could do that. Certainly would be something to look forward to."

Deb reached for the fancy bed and breakfast stationery, and the ball point pen masquerading as a fountain pen, that were on the night stand. She began writing. "Okay, highest point in each New England state. Where else?"

Tom looked hard at her. "Where else, what?"

Deb proclaimed, "A new list. A better list. Our other lists sucked. Interesting or off-the-wall places to have sex. Public places, so to speak. Not at home, not in a hotel. So, where else?"

Tom was a bit shocked. "You're serious?"

She continued thoughtfully writing. " . . . on a beach, in a plane, a train. In a taxi or Uber. Well, maybe that's too creepy, with the driver right there." She crossed that out as soon as she had written it. "I wish I had my extra long, legal pad now."

Tom stared at her paper and her growing list. "What are you talking about?"

She coaxed him, "Let's go. Help me out here. No, wait! I'm too hungry. Let's work on this at that tavern down the street. This will go better with a couple beers in us, especially for you. I've heard prudes need alcohol to loosen up." She laughed as she got up and slid the stationary and pen into her purse.

Tom was staring at her sideways as he stood and picked up his jacket.

Deb was smiling naughtily. "And by the way, you didn't stop me in the dressing room. As I recall, you owe me a dinner."

The charming tavern down the street was dimly lit and furnished entirely in dark wood, but homey and welcoming. There was a hum of light conversation but otherwise it was quiet in the dining room.

Tom and Deb were in a booth against the far wall. Two half empty glasses of amber beer were on the table, but no food. Deb took a sip of beer and continued to write with her pseudo-fountain pen.

She said, "The first nuclear submarine ever, the Nautilus, right in our back yard . . . somewhere in Foxwoods, and Mohegan Sun . . . on the trail in at least one state park, like Bluff Point. Or maybe in or around Gillette's Castle."

Tom proposed, "Fort Trumbull, in the fort. Oh, and Mystic Seaport, like maybe on the Morgan, or somewhere else famous or interesting. Like that sea captain's center chimney cape that looks just like my Nana's house, built in the 1700s."

Deb continued to write. "Good, good, those are good. The Morgan is good, a famous, wooden tall ship. It's nice to have you plugged in on this process, Chandler."

"Thank you. How many so far?"

Deb ran her finger along the paper. "About fifty."

"How and when are we supposed to carry out all these graphic displays of public fornication?"

She shrugged, "We'll work them in as we can. Anyway, it'll be more entertaining than watching a hundred and fifty baseball games on TV."

"A hundred and sixty-two."

"What?"

Tom laughed, "Nothing. I can't argue with that. And we'll see lots of the local sites and tourist attractions in New England. Up close and personal, so to speak."

Deb scanned her paper. "These are good. But we need some ultimate goal, like a grand finale." With a bad French accent, she added, "Une pièce de résistance, a Magnum Opus."

Tom considered what they had already written on their list. "On a plane? The world's first nuclear submarine? Those aren't grand enough?"

"Not bad. And Fenway Park is a good one, or Yankee Stadium. We need something so far-fetched, so hard to achieve, we may never be able to do it. Or, get in big trouble trying."

Tom thought for a while, then proposed, "In Fenway, but up on the Green Monster."

She tilted her head. "You mean up on the wall? During a game? How are we supposed to do that?"

"Hey, I'm just making your point. Sounds impossible, doesn't it?"

Deb's eyes narrowed and she grinned mischievously while nodding. "Way to get with the program, Chandler. On the Green Monster, at Fenway Park. That is a good one."

Deb wrote a bit more, then put down the pen with finality and raised her beer glass. "To Chandler's List, and all the adventure we'll have achieving it."

Tom raised his glass, and they clinked and took a sip. "I'll drink to that. And all the trouble we'll get into trying to achieve 'list items.'"

Deb drank lustily and exhaled. "I hope our food gets here soon. I'm hungry. And buzzed. My stomach is very empty."

Tom said, "Good thing we're not driving."

"Oh, you will be, once we get back in the room."

Tom understood her suggestive remark and added, "And you're going to get . . . buzzed, again. But this time, you're going to get buzzed by me."

Her eyes narrowed. "Whatever that means."

"We'll see."

Chapter 14

At the front desk of the B & B the next morning, Tom and Deb were standing with their suitcases on the floor nearby. Tom was leaning over the counter as he read a receipt, visibly upset. Deb's hands were on her hips as she impatiently stared at him.

The front desk receptionist was a sweet, grandmotherly woman, patiently waiting as Tom finished reading.

He finally said, annoyed, "Our rate quote was one forty a night with the internet coupon and our AAA rate. Why is the bill three sixty-nine for two nights?"

The receptionist pointed to the receipt and said very gently, "See, there is a city tax, a boarding tax, and eight per cent sales tax. If I don't add those to your bill, I'd have to pay them myself."

"The coupon said one-forty," Tom said.

She added, "Plus any applicable fees and taxes."

Deb interrupted with, "It's okay, Tom. Let's go."

Tom folded the receipt. "Seems like intentional deception."

The receptionist said apologetically, "I'm sorry about that. There's really nothing I can do. But otherwise, how was your stay with us?"

Tom looked at her with irritation, stuffed the receipt into his pocket, grabbed his suitcase handle and headed for the door. "More fun than having my spleen removed with a butter knife."

The receptionist said, shocked, "Oh dear! I'm so sorry!"

Deb pulled her suitcase to follow Tom. Over her shoulder, she said to her, "Our stay was fine. You have a lovely inn. Thank you so much."

As they drove, leaving Freeport, Tom clenched the steering wheel as Deb looked out the side window.

Deb said, "I can't believe you said that to a sweet old lady."

He snapped back, "Would you leave me alone. It's like fraud or something."

"Oh, come off it. She had nothing to do with it. You got the coupon online and it said fees and taxes right on it. I'm pretty sure she wasn't making up those charges to rip us off."

"It added almost a hundred bucks."

She shook her head, looking out the window. "Clearly, this is a First World Problem. But somehow, life will have to go on. Anyway, isn't our newly created list pretty much priceless?"

Three hours later, the Volvo wagon was driving along mostly empty I-395 in northern Connecticut. It was overcast, a cool gray day. The trees were still bare in early spring and the landscape was mostly drab and colorless.

Suddenly, Deb cried, "Get off this exit!"

Tom yanked the wheel to the right and headed down the exit ramp.

"What's wrong?" he asked, in a sudden panic.

Deb was looking at her iPhone GPS. "Jerimoth Hill is just a few miles down this road. Yeah, this is it, exit 41. Turn left here on 101.

Tom made the left turn and asked, "What in the world is Jerry Moth Hill? And why do we care?"

"The highest point in Rhode Island! It could be our first list item."

Tom asked, "The highest point in Rhode Island? I'm not really prepared for a hike. And I didn't know we were starting."

"We sort of already did at LL Bean. This will be our first, next one. So listen, if our list is real, and we're actually going to do it, we'd better get cracking."

Just off the shoulder of Route 101, a brown and white point-of-interest sign read:

Jerimoth Hill, States Highest Point, 812 Feet

The Volvo wagon pulled up just in front of the sign. There were no other cars parked on the road, and essentially no traffic anywhere in sight.

Tom shifted the car into park, looked around, and said, "What is this? Where is it? There's no mountain here."

Deb was reading her phone, and laughing. "This website says it's a couple hundred yards off the road, that way. And get this. The 'summit,' the highest point in the state, is five feet higher than this road. Five feet higher than where we're parked right now."

Tom turned to stare at her. "Five feet? That really does sound like a treacherous climb."

"Looks like, 'not being prepared for a hike' won't be an issue."

Tom seemed to be waiting for something else to happen. But soon he said, "Are we really going to do this?"

"Hell, yes, we're going to do this. Let's go."

Among moderately spaced trees, Tom and Deb were tentatively walking on a wide, very flat path covered with leaves and pine needles. A few pine trees were scattered among the bare oaks and birches. It was quiet, with no traffic sounds or even birds chirping.

Tom was looking around, listening. There was not much to see or hear, but it was by and large a nice spot of real estate. "This must be the road less traveled I've heard so much about."

"Easier to achieve the desired goal."

Tom spotted a house through the trees, not far from the road. He pointed and said quietly, "Uh oh, what about the people that live there?"

Deb feigned exaggerated annoyance. "Would you get with the program. The whole point is a bit of adventure, a bit of risk."

"The whole point? Seems like there are other goals to be achieved."

"Arjum."

"What?" he asked, not understanding what she said.

"As you say, 'it's in the Urban Dictionary.' Arjum. A sarcastic exclamation used to reply to an absurd or off-the-wall statement. I could say, 'whatever,' or, 'as if,' but arjum is more appropriate."

He looked at her dumbly.

A few minutes later, they were standing among trees on perfectly flat ground, reading a small, white cardboard sign tacked to a birch tree.

Tom was looking around. "Is this it? I don't get it." He pointed to, "That pile of dirt and moss over there looks higher than this spot."

Deb pointed a little further down. "Look, there's one of those geographic surveyor plaques, or whatever they're called."

They walked a few yards and looked down at the small brass plaque on a flat rock.

Deb read out loud, "'U.S. Coast and Geodetic Survey.' Yeah, that's what I meant."

"This spot doesn't look like anything. It's completely flat. I didn't expect a life or death climb of the Matterhorn, but I am so confused."

Deb stepped to him, leaned in and kissed him gently. "This is it. They put these plaques on the high points."

She kissed him passionately, clawing her hands across his jacket, then pushed him back against the closest tree. She reached down and quickly unbuttoned her jeans.

As he was kissing her, Tom was looking around with one open eye. There was a soft crack of a breaking twig, causing him to jump and pull away from the kiss. He anxiously looked around.

He whispered, "What was that? Someone's coming!"

Deb was laughing. "Come off it. It's a squirrel. Look!"

Twenty feet away, a gray squirrel was loping across the ground between trees. It reached one and leapt to the trunk, scurrying up.

Tom anxiously said, "Are you sure about this?"

Deb said seductively, "No one will be higher than us in Rhode Island for the next ten minutes."

She leaned in for a very deep, hard kiss.

Four Minutes Later

Deb was zipping up her jacket and then she fluffed leaf fragments and pine needles out of her hair. Tom adjusted his pants, rotating his hips slightly.

He said, "Man, I'm still bulging in here. These jeans don't fit again."

"If it lasts more than four hours, don't tell your doctor, tell me."

Tom was still not convinced they weren't being watched. After scanning the woods around them, he pointed, "Hey, wait. What's that clearing over there?"

Deb turned to look. "Uh oh. We'd better check it out."

They walked between trees, then off the path, towards the clearing. They soon stopped and read a small white sign tacked to a tree, exactly like the first one.

Tom looked around, but didn't see any geodetic survey markers. "Another one? What's up with that?"

A few steps later, they arrived in the clearing. It was covered with weeds and gravel, and there was a small shed off the back edge. To the right was a large flat rock the size of their kitchen table, three feet high. On it was a tall pile of smaller rocks, and yet another small white sign tacked to a nearby tree.

Deb looked around. "This might really be it. This pile of rocks is definitely higher than over there. I think we did it in the wrong spot."

Tom said, unimpressed and without commitment, "Bummer."

She said, "We'll have to do it here to be sure."

"Yeah, right." Then he saw that she was serious, and said, "Uh, I don't think that's going to happen. At least not for another ten or fifteen minutes."

Deb faced him and put her hands on her hips. "You have some other important business you have to attend to in the next twenty minutes?"

Tom shrugged.

Twenty-one or Twenty-two Minutes Later

Tom was buckling his jeans as Deb was pulling on her jacket.

She said, "Our first official list item. Congratulations, Chandler."

He behaved as if he had just received an Academy Award, turning and waving to the imaginary crowd. "You like me! You really like me!" He then said, "Oh, no, congratulations to you, Mrs. Chandler."

Deb and Tom climbed into either side of their Volvo. There were still no other cars nearby, but Tom looked guilty, searching ahead and behind, and towards the one visible house just into the woods.

Deb was watching him and said playfully, "You really are a prude."

"What can I say, my ancestors were Puritans. A couple were actually on the Mayflower."

"Oh, well, that certainly explains it, except for one minor detail." She paused and said, with severely exaggerated annoyance and dramatic pauses, "That was four hundred f-ing years ago!"

He looked at her and laughed, then started the car. He said, "That wasn't so bad. Jerimoth Hill, who knew. But what about Mount Washington? Or Katahdin in Maine? That's like a seven hour drive, and an all day hike up and down."

Deb nodded. "How about that. This could get very exciting."

The Volvo made a U-turn across the road, heading for home.

Chapter 15

In the cafeteria at SOEL Headquarters, Eric, who was now 37, and two relatively young engineers, Jeff and Scott, were eating around a table. Tom was eating with them, passively listening to their conversation with annoyance as they discussed an engineer in a different department.

Eric proclaimed, "Can you believe it? He was actually watching porn, on his laptop, in his cube."

Jeff asked, "Aren't those sites blocked by our cybersecurity?"

Eric said, "I know, right? He figured out a way to get around security. I don't know how. The site was, Throbbing Threesomes. I heard he'd been on it dozens of times. It's the first actual firing since Snore-tin' Morton, way back when. And Morton had to sleep every morning for twelve years before they canned his fat ass."

"Sorry I missed his reign," said Scott. "It must have been a thrill a minute."

"I almost forgot," Jeff said, "I have the new Bingo game sheets for our next meeting. I'll email everyone the PDF."

Tom looked up. "Bingo? You play Bingo in our meetings?"

Jeff feigned insult, "Bullshit Bingo. I've updated the score sheet to include a few of the hottest management buzzwords."

Scott cooed with high anticipation, "Ooo, tell me now. Please, please."

Jeff said, "Of course, win-win is always the free space. That has been said in every meeting since the Dawn of Man, and will be until Armageddon. 'Synergistic' and 'buy-in from key stakeholders' are still there, timeless classics. But we've added . . . wait for it . . . 'it's on my radar,' and 'helicopter view.' And then a couple great new additions that make you wonder, what took them so long to find their way back into the lexicon: 'Results driven,' 'I don't have the bandwidth' and, last but certainly not least, 'let's take this off line.'"

Scott said, "Supercalifragilisticexpialidocious! Pulling a couple of the classics back in. Yeah, I'd forgotten about those. Now I can anxiously look forward to our next meeting."

Tom looked down and took the last bite of his food.

Eric leaned back in his chair and extended his arms far apart. He said, "Guess what this is . . ." Then he loudly, proudly exclaimed, "I haven't taken a dump in three days!"

Tom looked up at him quietly.

Scott said, "Uh, I haven't the foggiest."

'A new HR training catchphrase?" asked Jeff.

Eric proudly said, "No. It's the Constipation Proclamation!"

At that, Tom stood. "I'll catch you guys later. I've got a meeting with the boss."

Jeff said, "Well, I hope you have a synergistic, win-win interlinkage with the key stakeholders."

Tom walked away with his tray, shaking his head.

A little while later, in Ashley's office, Tom was animated and explaining things enthusiastically. Ashley was listening closely.

"The technology is already established and in house. Actually, it's kind of old. Mostly just bar codes and scanners."

Ashley thoughtfully replied, repeating what he had been proposing. "So any equipment in the trail of ownership is scanned at transmission, and then again at receiving, and both managers' ID's are scanned at the same time?"

Tom nodded. "No paper forms at all. Automatically recorded and stored. Similar to UPS or Post Office tracking. Never a question where the equipment should be. The only real investment is bar-coding stickers to put on pieces of equipment that don't already have them. And downloading the software."

"Where do we get that?"

Tom spread his hands and shrugged, "Anywhere. It's ubiquitous and cheap. Several brands and versions."

Ashely considered briefly, "That's pretty good, Tom. The Procedure Proposal Form is filled out?"

"I'll have the PPF done by the end of the day tomorrow."

"Get it to me ASAP. I'll review it and move it forward."

"That would be great. Thanks."

She added, "And maybe fortuitously, this is the first year for that new performance review system. I have plenty to add for yours."

"What's that called again?" he asked.

"I'm pretty sure it's called, Corporate Review and Performance Summary."

Tom nodded passively and said, "Right, right," until suddenly something occurred to him. "Wait, did you say, 'Corporate Review and Performance Summary?' C, R, A, P, S?"

Ashley looked at him dumbly for a second, and then her green eyes opened wide. She burst out laughing, though Tom just smiled and shook his head. She said, "Our annual CRAPS Reports! How can we not call them that?"

"HR must have done that on purpose. Or someone really dropped the ball. Sort of amazing they would do that."

Ashley stopped smiling, and was studying him seriously. "Are you okay? You seem kind of tired."

"Yeah, I guess I am. Work and home life have been pretty demanding. The three kids keep us both really busy, and Deb has been working a lot of weekends and nights."

"That sounds exhausting. You haven't used any vacation this year. Got anything planned?"

Tom shrugged, "Not really. We have a couple long weekends tentatively planned. And we'll do something as a family in the summer, but we haven't finalized anything that far ahead."

"I guess I could use some time off myself. It's a long haul from MLK Day until Memorial Day. And I'm not feeling quite right. My back's been sore and I'm getting tingling in my fingers. Probably carpal tunnel. I'm on my laptop twelve hours a day."

"Yeah, I guess we all are."

Ashley stood, ending the meeting. "Get the PPF to me. If there's anything else you need, let me know."

Tom said with a genuine smile, "Just make sure you write me a good CRAPS report."

Ashley laughed out loud.

Chapter 16

A COUPLE WEEKS LATER

The Province Lands, a fraction of the National Seashore on the outer tip of Cape Cod, were largely undeveloped. The most significant human encroachment were paved bicycle trails that wound for miles through the protected sand dunes and beaches.

Deb and Tom were in sweaters, riding rented bicycles on the narrow, paved path. Tom was wearing a backpack, loaded with food, drinks and place settings for a picnic. They rolled up and down small hills, and around some sharp curves. Flashing by on either side were sprawling sand dunes and scattered clusters of scraggly pines and short, scrubby bushes. Frequently, small amber diamond-shaped signs flashed by, warning of steep hills and curves, exactly like miniature traffic signs. Since it was still early in the spring vacation season, no other riders were on the bicycle trails.

As they rode, there was a continuous clicking of the gear derailleurs, and a loud clacking sound, over and over.

Deb shouted ahead, "My pedal is hitting the kickstand!"

Tom called back over his shoulder, "Okay, we'll stop down this hill and I'll see if I can fix it."

Deb muttered to herself, "Of course, I get the crappy bike."

They coasted to the bottom of the hill and stopped.

After Tom adjusted the kickstand, they continued riding along at a leisurely pace. A little later, they arrived at their destination, Race Point Beach. The parking lot was empty as they slowly pedaled up the slight incline toward the ocean.

To the northwest, past the crest of the primary dune above the beach, the huge orange globe of the sun was several minutes from setting over the water. The surface of the ocean was a flat calm, reflecting the gold and amber, and a few light clouds like a shimmering mirror.

From the landward side, Tom and Deb rode their bicycles and stopped at the edge of the sand. They dismounted and quietly scanned the scene, up and down the beach. It was breathtaking.

Tom said reverently, "Look at the colors."

Deb added, "I don't think I've ever seen the ocean so calm in my life."

Tom's eyes were wide in wonder, glowing with the reflection of the sun on the water. He was slowly shifting his gaze until suddenly, he locked sight on something. He squinted slightly for better focus.

In absolute awe, he pointed and said quietly, "God, look out there, to the left. Is that what I think it is?"

Deb followed the direction of his finger, just to the right of the glowing sun. "Where?"

Out to sea, rhythmically arching through the water, was the rounded back and small dorsal fin of a whale. Starkly black against the gold and amber water, it moved silently, leaving an expanding wake on the otherwise perfectly flat ocean.

Deb quickly saw it and asked, "Oh my God, what is that? A dolphin?"

"It looks too big. It's probably a humpback whale. Wow. That is amazing."

"Wish we had the binoculars."

The whale continued to knife through the water, seemingly across the entire horizon from end to end. Tom and Deb watched in silent wonder for quite a while.

Moments later, to the left, the huge orange globe of the sun just touched the water.

Tom said solemnly, "That is quite a scene."

She said with resolution, "Let's have wine and cheese here. This is a really good list item."

The sun had set but a faint glow at the horizon remained to their left, and behind the beach. The air had cooled rapidly, but without any wind, it was a lovely evening.

The glowing remnants of a wood fire were in a small pit in the sand, built and left behind by someone else. Tom was poking a stick in the embers, stirring up sparks and smoke.

He said, "It was pretty nice of someone to leave this for us. We should be able to get it going again."

Deb called, "Here's a pile of dry driftwood. We can use this."

She walked closer to the pit and dropped a handful of small sticks on the sand between the fire and their small plaid blanket. Two plastic cups and an open wine bottle were next to blocks of cheese, crackers and a bunch of red grapes.

Tom dropped a few smaller wood pieces on the embers and poked around with the stick. Soon, fresh flames erupted in the pit.

"That'll keep it going for a while," he said.

Deb sat down on the blanket. Immediately her hands began moving back and forth under her sweater. Soon they withdrew, holding her black bra that she tossed aside. Though the lighting was dim, the contours of her breasts were clearly visible through the loose weave of her sweater.

She said, "Wine is refilled, cheese is ready."

Tom sat on the blanket near her. "Nice. Thanks."

The sand dunes up the beach were empty, and the crackling of the fire was the only sound. Half of the waxing moon was bright in the clear sky behind them.

Tom had finished chewing cheese and sipped wine from the plastic cup, gazing out at the last light over the water.

"It's so nice here."

Deb was peering at him with mild impatience. She looked down at her hardened nipples, pressing out against her sweater, and said, "Apparently, I'm cold."

"Oh, I'm sorry, do you want my . . ." Then he noticed. "Hey. What's all this? What's all this?"

"What do you think this is, a Boy Scout jamboree?"

Tom said, "It's not dark."

She rolled her eyes, "Are you starting that again? There's no one else here."

Deb gingerly moved his wine and cheese to one side, clearing most of the blanket. She crawled to him, forced him to his back, then climbed on top, kissing him hard on the mouth.

Six Minutes Later

Up the sand, car headlight beams framed the top of the dune in harsh white light. A car door clacked open, followed by a muffled voice, and then the high-pitched barking of a small dog. Soon the silhouette of the dog crested the dune in the glaring light and hurried down toward the water in shadows.

In the dark on the blanket, there was frantic swishing of clothing, a belt buckle clanking, and muffled, incoherent swearing.

Quickly, the brown, mottled, basenji scurried up to Tom and Deb, leaping and darting playfully around the blanket.

As Deb buttoned her jeans, she said, "Hey little guy. Aren't you the cutest thing."

Tom wasn't quite as excited to see the basenji, and was having trouble buttoning his ill-fitting jeans, yet again.

The male voice of the basenji owner called from the top of the dune. "Zoey! Here, Zoey! Here, girl!"

Zoey stopped at his voice, and her ears perked up. But then, while standing still, she smelled the cheese and quickly scurried the few steps toward the blanket.

Still trying to close his jeans, Tom blocked Zoey with an arm. "Oh, no, I don't think so."

Zoey's owner approached in the shadows and walked into a bit of dim light. "Sorry about that. She's really friendly."

Urgently, Tom rolled to his side, facing away from Zoey's owner.

Deb said quickly, "No problem. She's adorable."

Zoey's owner was able to grasp her collar, pull her close to him, and clip on a leash. "We're just heading down the beach. Beautiful evening, isn't it?"

Deb said, "Yes, lovely. Have a good walk."

Tom and Deb sat up and watched as their silhouettes faded down the beach in the dim light.

After a while, Deb said with a smile, "That was a close one."

To Deb's surprise, Tom said without protest, "We'd better get cracking before they come back."

Deb looked at him happily, though he couldn't see her expression, and said, "Right. At least once."

They moved together and kissed, reclining back on the blanket.

A couple hours later into the evening, they were riding their bicycles back along the same winding, paved trail. Deb's bike was rolling without clacking as she followed Tom, who rode twenty feet ahead. Though it was night and they were on the narrow, winding path, they moved along at a normal bike-riding speed. The white sand of the dunes seemed to glow in the moonlight, accented by the silhouettes of the pine trees.

Tom called back to her, "It's amazing how easy it is to see, just from the moonlight. We should be back at the inn in a little while."

Deb called ahead, "I can feel sand grinding against the seat in my hoo-hoo."

Tom grimaced, "Ouchies. Hopefully three times at that list item was worth it."

"I'll let you know after I've had a shower."

The two bicycles rode in tandem over the crest of a dune and coasted easily down the next hill.

Chapter 17

The front door of the Chandler house opened and Tom and Deb walked in to see Kaitlyn laying on the couch with a sheet over her body, remaining perfectly still. Kevin was kneeling on the floor in front of her.

Deb rolled her suitcase to the side, calling, "Hi guys! What are you doing?"

Kevin turned to them and called, "Playing Wake!"

Deb was confused. "Wake? That's a game? How do you play?"

Kevin said proudly, "I invented it. This time, Kaity is the guest of honor."

"Game over. Mommy! Daddy!" cried Kaitlyn, jumping off the sofa.

Kaitlyn ran over to them and hugged Deb around the waist. Emily walked in from the kitchen.

Deb's nose sniffed the air and crinkled up. "Whoa, what is that? It smells like . . . dirty feet."

As Kevin walked closer, Deb's sense of smell narrowed down the source of the fetid aroma to him. "Kevin, is that you?"

Kevin stopped a few feet away, didn't answer, and looked very guilty.

"Kevin? What is that? Is that your feet?"

Reluctantly, he gave in and explained. "I bet Jason at school I could wear the same pair of socks longer than him! I'm winning!"

In her head, Deb swore, but said, "I really hate to ask, but how long have you been wearing those same socks?"

After a moment, Kevin said, "78 days in a row. But I don't wear them to bed! Please don't make me take them off!"

Tom was just inside the door and said, "Right now, Kevin. Upstairs and put them right in the washing machine. I can smell them from the door, and I'm ten feet away."

"I'm sure!" Reluctantly, he trudged upstairs.

Deb watched him with concern, but asked, "Other than that, how did everything go?"

Kaitlyn announced, "We got an Old Faithful pizza!"

Tom set down his suitcase. "Great! Any left for us?"

Emily had a serious expression and said, "Mom, Grandma called a few times. She wanted you to call her as soon as you got home."

"Did she say what was happening?"

"Not really," Emily said. "She sounded really confused, and didn't really remember that she already called."

"She could have called my iPhone. Did you make sure she had that number?"

"Every time she called I told her. It was like she didn't understand. And definitely didn't remember."

Deb hugged her, "Okay, thanks. I'll call her in a little while."

Deb and Tom were sitting on their bed later that evening, after Deb had called Lynn.

Tom asked, "Did I hear right? She said something about the police? What happened?"

"She was driving home from her polka dancing, like she has a hundred times, and got lost."

"She got lost on the way home from dancing?"

"She was parked on the side of the road for a long time, trying to figure it out. Eventually a cop stopped and helped her. He looked at her license, put her address in her GPS, and escorted her home."

"That was awfully nice of him." Tom noticed she was very distracted and concerned. "I'm so sorry."

"Thanks."

Tom sighed slowly. "It's kind of amazing how we get forty-eight hours of peace, and then crash and burn back to reality."

She turned on him with anger. "This isn't about us, ass! My mother's dementia may have gotten critical!" She looked away, shaking her head.

"I'm sorry, you're right. What can we do for her now?"

"I don't know. She's going to have to be evaluated in detail. She might not be able to live in her house anymore. Having to move would really hurt her."

Tom thought a second. "Why don't you visit her. Be there for emotional support when she's evaluated. Work on a plan if she needs to move to a senior community. Make calls with her, visit places, whatever she needs."

"Drive to Ohio alone?"

"Sure, if you're up for that. Next Sunday is Mother's Day. Get there Wednesday, be there for her evaluation, visit some local retirement communities, stay through the weekend."

Deb thoughtfully considered the logistics of that. "That actually could help her a lot. You'd be okay with stuff here? Getting them off to school and everything else?"

"It was my suggestion, wasn't it? The kids and I will make it work."

"My only work scheduled this weekend is the vendor show at the convention center Saturday. I can probably find someone who would love to take that shift for me."

Tom said, "Great, it's settled. I'll talk to the kids and we'll figure out school and work logistics, meals and stuff."

Deb breathed a sigh of relief. She turned and smiled at him. "Thanks for suggesting that. That would probably help a lot."

"No problem."

"I doubt it's Alzheimer's, but it may not be safe for her to live alone anymore."

She leaned in and kissed him lightly and they hugged for a long time.

Deb had left for Ohio very early Wednesday morning. It was hectic, and Tom was late getting everything together, but he got the kids off to school that morning and managed to survive in one piece.

Several engineers, including Eric, Jeff and Scott, were in their same conference room around the table. Ashley was standing in front of a Power Point slide projected on the white board, holding a remote control with a laser pointer. The slide only showed '5-S' in large block letters on a bright white background.

The door in the back of the room opened quietly. Tom tried to slink in without being noticed, but Ashley stopped talking and looked at him. He sat in the chair closest to the door, looking a bit mortified because he was late.

Tom said quietly, "Sorry. I had to get the kids off to school by myself."

Ashley said, "No worries, Tom. We were just getting started." She spoke louder, to everyone. "As I was saying, it's time for our annual 5-S refresher, required by HR."

There was a visible slumping of posture and shifting of positions in the room, and a muffled chorus of sighs. Ashley pressed a button on the remote to display a new slide. It had the same large block letters on a white background and only said:

STREAMLINE   SORT   SHINE   STANDARDIZE   SUSTAIN

Ashley said, "Yes, here they are again, the five S's. I'm going to start with 'streamline' today." She clicked the remote and the slide went dark. She put down the remote, closed her laptop, and powered off the projector. She then continued with, "This presentation has just been streamlined. That's all I'm going to say about the five S's during this meeting."

There was a visible stirring in the room.

"All our schedules are crammed," she continued. "Our time is valuable, and it's rare we can all get together. I want to use this next . . . seventy-nine minutes, to talk about ways we can improve our processes. And brainstorm about any new ideas you might have."

Tom settled back in his seat, gave a short fist-pump and silently mouthed an enthusiastic, 'yes!'

Ashley continued, "And we need to discuss the parameters of our new performance review process, the Corporate Review and Performance Summary." She looked at Tom and smiled. "Which has already affectionately been dubbed, 'CRAPS Reports.'"

Jeff and Scott noticed her eye contact with Tom, and made eye contact with each other. Under the table, Scott made a circle with his thumb and index finger, and rapidly thrust his other index finger in and out of the hole.

Chapter 18

In the Chandler back yard, the oak trees were budding with fresh, green leaves against a dazzling blue sky. Scattered, puffy, white cumulus clouds were racing on high winds. It was a beautiful spring day.

Tom was crouching like a catcher, setting a target with his baseball glove. A ball bounced in to him that he trapped deep in the ankle-high grass. Standing, he threw it gently back, then motioned with his hand as he described correct throwing mechanics.

"Bring the ball right up behind your ear, keep your head straight, and bring your arm forward. Now watch Kevin do it this time." He crouched again.

Kevin and Kaitlyn were standing side by side, both wearing baseball gloves and Red Sox caps, thirty feet from him across the yard.

Kevin reached into the pocket of his shorts and pulled out a doll head, just about the same size as the baseball they were throwing. He wound and threw. The doll head, hair trailing like a comet tail, flew through the air. Tom caught it with surprise, and examined it.

Kaitlyn knew immediately and complained, "Hey! That's my Betty Lou! You took off her head!"

Tom put the doll head in his own pocket. "Kevin, please. Behave."

Kevin was still smirking. "Sure, Dad. But how was my throw?" He turned and grinned at Kaitlyn mischievously.

Tom said with more impatience, "Kevin!"

Kevin wound and threw the baseball with a good motion. Tom easily caught it.

Tom said, "See, Kaity, keep your elbow closer to your body and throw straight ahead from behind your ear."

Deb's voice suddenly called from near the house, "Important business, I see. While the grass still hasn't been mowed."

Kaitlyn yelled, "Mommy!"

"Hi Mom," said Kevin.

Deb was standing on the back deck, setting down a small travel bag. Kaitlyn ran up the steps and jumped into her arms.

Deb hugged Kaitlyn, while she said, "Mmm, hi sweetie. It's good to be home."

Tom walked toward the house. "Hi. How was your drive?"

She said quickly, "Awful. Can we talk inside, when you're finished?"

Deb was standing in their bedroom, her partially unpacked bag on the bed. Tom was sitting in the chair in the corner of the room.

He said with annoyance, "Come on. Kevin wanted to play catch, and Kaity wanted me to teach her to throw better. Is the lawn more important than that?"

Deb said, "I'll get stuck doing it during the week."

"It's grass, not an emergency appendectomy. It can wait a few days."

Deb sighed, conceding. "Okay, okay. Traffic was awful. It was stop and go from Norwalk to Branford. And the f-ing GW is always a mess. I should just drive the fifty extra miles and take I-84."

Tom asked sincerely, "Did you get any kind of diagnosis from your mom's evaluation?"

"Nothing definitive. They really won't try to make any final conclusion until the end of the week."

"Why so long?"

Deb said, with a hint of impatience, "It's complicated with dementia. There's really not a definitive test, but it's likely not Alzheimer's. We've got no family history or anything like that."

"That would be better, I suppose. How's she doing?"

"She's scared, when she understands what's happening, but most of the time she's just doing her same old stuff. She was mad when we talked about maybe she shouldn't be driving. And upset that she'll likely need to move. She loves her 'gold mine' house. Even though in reality the house itself has always been more of a 'tear-down.'"

"It sounds like she really should not be driving. Did you get to visit any senior centers?"

"We went to a couple. Sebring Pines about twenty miles from her house seemed really good. One looked like they were more or less warehousing old people until they died. That was really depressing. Sebring has a service to help with moving, too." Deb pulled clothes out of her bag and walked to the dresser, fitting them back into a drawer. "I'm really tired. We can talk more later. I just want to shower and go to bed early."

Tom tried to change the subject. "This week, maybe even tomorrow, you need a list item."

Deb walked back to her travel bag, looking down, "Honestly, that doesn't sound very tempting right now. Maybe I'll feel better after a good night's sleep. You actually think we can do something on a weekday?"

Tom said playfully, "I've never . . . launched . . . on a submarine before. You could pick me up for lunch."

Deb rolled her eyes. "How could any girl resist such a sweet offer?"

It was raining lightly as the Volvo splashed through small puddles and pulled into the empty parking lot at Nautilus Park.

Inside the USS Nautilus, the world's first nuclear submarine, there was a long double flight of gleaming, metal stairs. Plexiglas walls protected the displayed controls and equipment on either side.

Tom and Deb arrived at the top of the stairs. They slowly descended, glancing from side to side, until they reached the bottom. As they stepped onto the steel floor, large, green torpedoes behind the Plexiglas came into view.

Deb looked around and said, "Is this really where the torpedoes were stored? Guys just worked in here crammed into space right in the middle of a bunch of bombs?"

Tom, who designed submarine systems for a living, said, "Everything on these ships was fit into as little available space as possible. This is the first one ever built with nuclear power, so they were trying to be hyper-efficient. They hadn't come close to perfecting personal space ambiance for the sailors."

"Yikes," she said. "Maybe my job isn't so bad."

They walked a few more steps and stood in front of a small control room behind Plexiglas. It was currently being operated by two mannequins, wearing loose uniforms and navy hats.

Tom looked back up the stairs, then the other direction down a short hallway. Since it was a weekday, this educational and historic tourist site was presently void of any other visitors.

Tom asked evenly, "So, do you want to get torpedoed in the torpedo room?"

Deb faked acting smitten. "Aw, that is so romantic. Right in front of these sailors?" She motioned at the mannequins.

"If they don't like it, they can cover their eyes. So now who's the prude?"

Tom grabbed her shoulders gently, kissed her hard, and slowly forced her back against the Plexiglas. After a few seconds, he turned her around quickly so her front was pushed against the glass. He kissed the back of her neck and reached around to unbutton her jeans.

A view from inside the control room revealed Deb's face pressed against the clear wall, eyes closed, with her body and head rhythmically moving back and forth. Soon her eyes opened, at first not looking at anything in particular, intensely feeling what was happening. But when she finally locked gaze on something, her eyes widened and she was suddenly uncomfortable.

Through the glass in the control room, a few feet from her, were the two mannequins. Her quick glances at their faces revealed, quite clearly, that they both appeared to be smirking wryly, and were thoroughly amused by what was happening in front of them.

Chapter 19

The doorbell rang in the Chandler house. Tom stood quickly from the couch and walked to the front door. The play-by-play announcing of a Red Sox game was on the television.

Tom opened the door to greet Doug Wilson, Emily's friend, who was nearing the end of his junior year in high school. He was clean cut, with boyish good looks, wearing jeans and a designer golf shirt. He and Tom shook hands.

Tom smiled, "Hi Doug, good to see you again."

Doug said warmly, "Hey Mr. Chandler. Is Em ready?"

"Come on in for a second." Tom motioned to the living room. "I think she's upstairs. I'll go check."

"Thanks."

Doug walked into the living room and waited quietly, watching the game passively on the television. Tom climbed the stairs to check on Emily.

Suddenly, Kevin ran into the living room from the kitchen. He was chasing a fly as it zigzagged across the room. It finally landed on the shade of the lamp in the corner nearest the television.

Kevin paused when he saw it land, stealthily moving closer. The fly crawled around on the shade, unaware. Kevin raised a rubber band that had been cut into a straight strand. He stretched it back with one hand and moved his other hand closer, closer, taking steady aim just a few inches from the fly.

At just the right spot, he suddenly released the stretched end of the rubber band. Thwack! The fly was vaporized, leaving only a burgundy smudge on the lampshade.

Doug had been watching. "Nice shot."

Kevin said, "Thanks. I'm getting better."

"Last year, my brother and I spent the better part of the summer hunting flies and other bugs like that."

Kevin was impressed. "You must have gotten pretty good."

"We did. But now he has a real job, and I'm going to start working at Buttonwoods Farm in a couple weeks. You know, the ice cream stand. No more fly hunting for us." He shook his head and laughed. "That probably wasn't our most productive summer ever."

Tom trotted down the stairs. "She'll be down in a second. So, what's the plan for tonight? A movie?"

Doug said, "Nine fifteen show in Waterford. Emoji Movie III. It looks cute."

Tom shook his head. "Another Emoji Movie?" He thought to himself, has Hollywood completely run out of ideas?

Doug was quiet for a second, watching the game.

Tom noticed him watching and asked, "Are you a Sox fan?"

"Yeah, my whole family is, for as long as I can remember. And Mike just got a job interning with the team for the summer."

Tom recalled meeting Mike Wilson. "Your brother, right. What does he do as an intern?"

Doug said, "Mostly phone and online ticket sales at Fenway. It's a low position, but a good resume thing. Foot in the door with the team and all that."

Tom started to speak, but footfalls rushing down the stairs interrupted him. Kaitlyn ran into the living room.

Excited, Kaitlyn squealed, "Hi Dougie!"

Doug said politely, "Hey, squirt."

She rushed over and hugged him around the waist. Emily walked down the stairs, just behind Kaitlyn.

Emily gushed, "Hi!"

A bit shyly, Doug said, "Hi, Em."

Tom asked Doug, "Does Mike actually work at Fenway?"

"Yeah, phones mostly, up in the offices. He keeps telling us if we ever need tickets, he could hook us up. He could get us into the park early. See behind the scenes, and other stuff."

Tom's interest was suddenly aroused. "What kind of stuff?"

Emily was becoming annoyed. "Dad, quit it."

Doug was happy to talk about it. "On the field for batting practice near home plate, maybe even up to the broadcast booth on certain days. Stuff like that."

Emily insisted, "We should get going."

"That's good to know," said Tom. "Thanks, Doug."

Emily pulled Doug by the arm toward the front door. "We'll be late."

"We'll be back by twelve," Doug called back.

"Okay, you two," said Tom. "Drive smart. Have fun."

Kaitlyn said, very sweetly, "Bye, Dougie."

Emily rolled her eyes as she and Doug headed out and closed the front door behind them.

Kevin muttered, though Tom couldn't hear him, "It's amazing what you can snag on an empty hook."

Tom watched them go, thinking, behind the scenes at Fenway. Interesting, very interesting.

Tom was sitting at his cubicle, his back to his monitors that were ablaze with schematics and data. Eric, Scott and Jeff were standing there, talking to him.

Tom said, "No, thanks. I'll just eat up here. I've got a meeting with Ashley in a little while."

Scott said, "Trying to be the teacher's pet?"

Tom's eyes narrowed. "She proposed the meeting."

Jeff said in a mocking tone, "Ooo, mister hoity-toity. Begging for doggie treats, teacher's pet?"

Eric added, "Who wouldn't want to be her pet."

Tom just looked at them without reaction, turned back to his monitors, and began hitting his keyboard. They walked away jabbering like monkeys.

Tom knocked on the door of Ashley's office. After a brief pause she called from inside, "Come on in."

Tom opened the door and walked in. Ashley had just blown her nose into a tissue, quickly tossing it in the can under her desk. Her eyes were red and irritated. Tom noticed.

He walked over and sat in the chair. "Hey, what's up? You okay?"

"No, not really. Sorry, just give me a second." Ashley was close to crying again, and exhaled loudly.

Tom's concern grew. "Bad news for me?"

Ashley's mood quickly leveled off, and she was surprised he was thinking along those lines. "Oh, God no, nothing like that at all. You've been kicking ass the last couple months. Look, I just found this out a little while ago. I'll tell you, but no one else here knows, so keep it that way for now."

Tom became even more anxious. "What?"

Ashley exhaled. "I just got diagnosed with MS. The doctor called me a few minutes ago to confirm."

Tom felt a twinge in his chest. "Oh, no. Ashley, I am so sorry."

She lowered her head, fighting off tears. Tom essentially jumped out of the chair and slid around the desk. She stood and they embraced, but after a few seconds they awkwardly separated, not making eye contact. Tom backed away a couple steps but remained standing next to the desk.

"Thanks," she said. "I shouldn't be acting this way at work, being a supervisor and all."

Tom dismissed that comment out of hand. "Are you kidding? That's huge news. You should take the rest of the day off." He let her catch her breath for a few seconds. "Do you have symptoms?"

"I stopped nursing Brittany six months ago. Seems like a few things have been creeping in gradually since then. Remember a few weeks back I had that tingling in my fingers? And my back was sore? It's gotten worse."

Tom asked rationally, "Are they sure it's MS?"

"I had a full body MRI. There are lesions in my spine, and at least one in my brain. They're small, but they are definitely there. The diagnosis is pretty certain."

"I am so sorry. I don't know anything about treatments for that. What is there?"

"My doctor will figure that out this week." She paused a second and looked up at him. "By the way, the reason I proposed this meeting wasn't to tell you this. I wanted to let you know, I've put you in for a promotion."

Tom was genuinely surprised. "Oh! Great! Thanks!"

"You deserve it. Whatever you've been doing the past couple months, eating differently, exercising, whatever, you've been like a different person. Just keep it up."

Tom smiled as he realized the double-meaning of the pun, but didn't let her in on his secret. "I intend to keep it up."

Ashley continued, "It's essentially a lock, but the review committee won't finalize it for several weeks. There will eventually be an announcement, but I'll keep you posted before that."

Tom watched her for a second, with a mixture of admiration and sympathy. He thought, she is definitely not just another pretty face, but said, "Thanks, Ashley. Let me know if there's anything I can do for you."

She finally smiled. "Just keep making my job easier, like you have been."

Chapter 20

Fort Trumbull in New London, Connecticut was originally built during the American Revolutionary War, and rebuilt and enhanced in the 1800's. Its solid stone and masonry structure was on top of a grassy hill, overlooking the half mile wide Thames River.

On the western bank of the Thames, two thousand people covered the hillside, clustered in small groups and families on blankets and chairs. The surface of the river was covered with dozens of boats. They ranged in size from tiny dinghies to majestic yachts and party boats, all anchored to hold firm against the current flowing south to Long Island Sound. All had gathered to watch the annual fireworks display.

Tom sat on a folding beach chair half way up the hill. Emily was in a chair next to him, her face buried in her iPhone. A blanket on the grass in front of them was covered with snack foods, drinks and games.

On one end of the blanket, Kaitlyn and Kevin were playing a game. White, red and green cards, each with a letter, were laid out in groupings on the blanket to form words.

Kevin looked from his hand to the cards on the blanket, and said in a low, sinister growl, "I just gotta find a way to make Kait lose."

Kaitlyn called out, "Dad, Kevin is playing stupid."

Kevin was quick to point out, "I didn't break any rules."

Tom asked, "What are you guys playing?"

"Wordplay," said Kaitlyn. "I made 'P-E-N' with my cards. And then Kevin just put down an I and S to make a wordplay from it."

Tom said, "Kevin, play politely."

"Hey, I made BUT, and then she used another T for a wordplay!"

Tom grumbled to himself, "The guy said that game would be educational." To the kids, he said, "Those are both real words, so you get the points. But please play politely."

Just then, a small gust of wind blew a few of the cards off the blanket, disrupting their game.

Kevin reached for them to try and hold them down, but couldn't grab them in time. Inadvertently, he muttered, "Shit."

Kaitlyn burst out laughing. "Dad!"

It was all Tom could do to keep from laughing himself, but said, "Kevin, please. You know better."

Emily looked up from her phone. "Mom should be here. This sucks."

"Yeah, her working on weekends is getting pretty old." He looked back at Fort Trumbull on top of the hill. The twenty foot high masonry fortress was a list item. He frowned. "For a few reasons, she should be here."

Emily said, "She just texted me that she's not getting home until one."

"I got that, too. Hey, where's Doug?"

"His family is at the Cape."

Tom was watching the boats on the river. "You excited about being a sophomore?"

Emily looked up at him. "Dad! For real? It's the 4th of July and you're asking me about school in two months?"

He conceded, "Sorry, sorry. Yeah, point taken."

"I can't wait to get my license, I'll tell you that."

Tom thought, very loudly in his own mind, 'Holy shit!'

In the clear night sky, fireworks continuously exploded with sequential cracks and very loud booms. Red, white and blue flares blew apart to form stars, hearts, smiley faces, and other shapes. In the distance, through tinny speakers, a patriotic song was playing, choreographed to the visual display above.

More fireworks exploded, filling the sky with descending trails of glittering tinsel that looked like a giant, gold willow tree.

Kaitlyn, covering her ears, snuggled against Tom's shirt. He tightened his arm around her as she flinched in reaction to each loud boom.

Kaitlyn whined, "They're too scary!"

Tom said comforting her, "Just a few more minutes."

Kevin and Emily were laying on the blanket side by side, contentedly watching the show. The conspicuously empty beach chair was on the grass next to Tom.

Now even sadder, Tom looked from the chair, back to the fort, then up at the fireworks flashing in the sky.

A few nights later, Tom and Deb parked on the street and then walked through the huge wrought iron gate at the entrance of the Connecticut College Arboretum. Visible in the sporadic glow of street lamps up and down the road, the branches of the trees surrounding the gate swayed slightly in the breeze, creating dancing shadows. A fence made of ten-foot-high iron bars lined the edge of the Arboretum near the road, in both directions.

Deb said, "It doesn't look like anyone is here."

"There shouldn't be, in the middle of summer in the evening. I think there's a stone bench we can, uh . . . use . . . further in."

They continued into the Arboretum, stepping lightly along the stone walkway and down a wide pathway on the grassy hill lined with trees and shrubs.

Ten Minutes Later

In the silent darkness on the bench, the barely visible silhouettes of Tom and Deb moved rhythmically.

Up the hill from them suddenly, the loud creaking of metal hinges pierced the silence, followed by several separate tones of metallic banging and clanking.

Tom and Deb stopped moving instantly.

Deb looked up the hill toward the sounds in the darkness. "What was that?"

Tom's heart sank. "Oh no, it couldn't be. I sure hope it's not what it sounded like."

In the darkness, they adjusted and fastened clothing and hurried up the walkway.

The now-closed gate was wrapped with a pad-locked, thick iron chain, securely holding both doors in place. There was no one visible in the glow of the street lamps.

Deb cried, "You have got to be shitting me. We're locked in?"

Tom said quickly, "I'll yell for whoever locked it."

"No!" Deb quickly exclaimed. "I don't want to explain what we're doing in here, now, at night!"

Tom was not convinced that was important, but said, "Okay. We'll try to find another way out."

12 Minutes Later

Tom and Deb were standing at a section of fence among the trees.

He said, "This fence must go on and on, maybe around the whole property."

She was very annoyed. "Now what? Camp out all night? Call 911, or the kids? Maybe Doug and Emily can pick us up." She shook her head. "I'm sure that won't be too embarrassing."

Tom had his hands on his hips and said, very sarcastically, "Uh, honey-bunny, poopsie, schnookums, let's try to be a little more productive here. There's got to be a way over it. Or through it." He walked a few steps further down, examining the fence line. He finally pointed. "Look at that branch." A thick branch extended far over the top of the fence, from a tree outside the enclosure, drooping within five feet of the ground.

Deb asked with deep reservations, "What about that branch?"

"We can climb out on it, and then shimmy over the fence."

"Like hell we can. I can't do that!"

Tom looked at her and teased. "No? Miss 'I'm in such good shape from all my work?' Come on, I'll help you get up."

Very reluctantly, Deb followed him to the branch. As he was hoisting her up, and she struggled to get a grip and maintain her balance, she muttered under her breath.

"Places that can't be locked while we're in them, from now on."

Chapter 21

At the entrance to the family owned orchard, a small wooden farm stand stood next to an opening in a wire fence framed with wooden posts. Behind the fence was a field of high bushes, thick with leaves and blueberries. Ali, the attendant working in the stand, was just there for the summer between semesters. She had long, strawberry blond hair, and was leaning on the counter next to a flat, metal produce scale. Bored, she was watching random videos on her iPhone. On the ground in front of the stand were several stacks of small, white buckets, each lined with a clear, plastic bag.

A hand printed sign was nailed to one post at the entrance to the field.

Blueberries - pick your own - $3.15 / lb

Tom and Deb suddenly appeared in the field between bushes and exited through the opening in the fence. They approached the farm stand in a bit of a hurry, each carrying one of those white buckets. They removed the plastic bags containing blueberries and placed them on the counter near Ali.

She said, with a smile. "How'd it go? Did you pick us clean?"

Ali adjusted their bags up on the scale, and then hesitated a moment. She noticed there were hardly any berries in their bags.

Ali said, "Oh. That is . . . six-tenths of a pound. Wasn't the picking good? You were back there for a while."

Tom and Deb looked guilty, not making eye contact with her.

Deb finally said, "Picking was fine. The bushes are loaded."

Ali laughed, "Did you get lost?"

Tom said, "We just need . . . a few."

"For muffins!" followed Deb, much too quickly.

Ali looked at them for a second and shrugged. She adjusted the bags again, read the scale, and said, "That's two dollars and three cents, with tax."

Tom gave her three one dollar bills, saying, "Keep the change."

Tom and Deb were sitting at the kitchen table with glasses of white wine. Their expressions were serious.

He said, "I'm pretty tired of it, too."

"I do what I can with the kids during the week."

"In summer you can do that. But when they're back in school, you'll never see them. If we're both out of the house now, they can take care of themselves. So if we're not with them for an hour or two, it doesn't matter. We're overdue trying to find you a day job."

"Yeah, I know. I'm keeping an eye out online for something, but I just don't have recent, relevant experience."

Tom thoughtfully said, "There are always admin openings at SOEL. I can look on the website."

Deb said, surprised, "Be a secretary for you?"

"Not necessarily in my department. There are lots of departments that probably have openings."

"And what, commute together?"

"I guess so, when we can, sure. I know you don't want to think about it, but Em will be driving early next year. She can help with errands, and drive Kevin and Kaitlyn places."

Deb took a long, deep drink of wine. "Oh god, don't even remind me. If we thought potty training was stressful, I can't wait to teach them to drive." She gasped. "Especially Kevin. That's going to be more fun than should be legal."

"True that. If I hear about job openings, do you want to apply?"

She took another quick drink. "Yeah. I will. It's time."

"It'll keep our options open."

Deb suddenly realized something and turned to him. "But don't think your cubicle is getting added to our list!"

"Oh, that would not be a good idea. We would both get fired. And that would be decidedly inconvenient."

The next morning, Tom and Ashley were meeting in her office.

Ashley smiled, "Sure! I'd be happy to ask around. We're doing a lot of hiring for all kinds of positions."

Tom said, "That'd be great. Thanks."

"I'd like to get to know Deborah better. The few times we've met, I didn't really get to talk to her that much. She seemed, I don't know, distant. I guess I just don't know her."

Tom looked away, and after a few seconds he tried to change the subject and said, "Hey, how are you? Any symptoms? Any treatment plans yet?"

"I feel about the same. They want me to start injections."

"Of what?"

"Copaxone. I can self-inject three times a week."

"That sounds inconvenient," he said

"Gilenya is a possibility, once a day oral, but it's, it's . . . wait for it . . . fifteen thousand dollars for three months' worth of pills."

Tom's jaw literally dropped.

Ashley smiled, and pulled back her long, red hair. "Insurance will cover almost all of that. Either way, I'll just have to deal with it all. Copaxone is the safest choice for anyone who might get pregnant. But of course, the best protection from MS symptoms is actually being pregnant."

Tom said, "I didn't know being pregnant had anything to do with preventing MS symptoms. Are you guys planning more kids?"

"We haven't decided. You tell me. How is it with three so close together in age?"

Tom was quiet for a few seconds, seriously considering. "You know, it used to be overwhelming, and it was a lot of stress, especially with our work schedules. But this year, well, Deb and I have worked more together on some things. It's been better, especially the last few months."

Chapter 22

Mystic Seaport, a village of original historic buildings and sites, filled the eastern bank of the Mystic River. Several old ships were moored at wooden docks, and the Mystic Drawbridge spanned the river just to the south. Several smaller privately owned kayaks, canoes and sailboats dotted the slow moving river north of Mystic.

In the Seaport, a gravel road along the Mystic River was lined with beautifully restored, early 19th century buildings. Three towering wooden masts rose skyward behind a long wooden wharf. The scene could have been straight out of the early 1800's, except for the clothes of the tourists who covered the wharf, and slowly meandered up and down the road.

The Chandler family was walking in the middle of this road. Kaitlyn was skipping along in front, with Kevin walking beside her. Tom and Deb were holding hands, strolling casually, looking at the sites on both sides. Emily was lagging behind, her nose to her phone.

They soon approached a staff member dressed as a pirate, greeting guests that passed him. Standing in the road, he wore an old-fashioned, sea-faring costume consisting of a striped shirt and black pants. An eye patch and a fake parrot on his shoulder completed the ensemble. He grinned widely and addressed them enthusiastically with an exaggerated pirate's brogue.

"Ahoy, mateys! Are ya havin' a jolly good day at the Seaport?"

Kevin and Kaitlyn giggled and walked over to him.

Kaitlyn said enthusiastically, "Yes!"

He called, "Shiver me timbers! That be great! I've a discount coupon for the gift shop. Twenty gold nuggets when ya' buy any treasure there. But I needs one of ya to tell me a joke, don't ya know!"

Kevin piped up immediately, "I know a joke! I made it up!"

The pirate was delighted. "Avast! Let's have it!"

Tom and Deb looked at each other with grave concern.

Kevin said, "Knock, knock!"

"Who be there?"

"Elephant!"

The pirate was excited, and of course expectantly said, "Elephant who?"

With delight, Kevin said, "Elephant cut off my skin!"

The pirate's expression collapsed completely. He looked at Kevin with dull astonishment, then complete confusion. But he held out the discount coupon, mumbling, "Thanks to ya for such a rousing good yarn."

Kevin excitedly took the coupon and waved it around, announcing, "Twenty dollars off!"

Emily looked up long enough to say, annoyed, "That wasn't a joke. That was just messed up."

The Pirate walked on, stunned, mumbling quietly, adjusting his eye patch. Past him, further down, a mortified Deb soon caught sight of the tall ship masts towering above the wharf. She nodded that way, and pulled Tom's arm.

"Hun, that ship is the Morgan."

Emily cried, "No more boats!"

Tom said to Emily, "This is the Seaport. Boats are generally the whole reason why it is here."

Emily said, "No! Can we please go to the gift shop now?"

Kevin chimed in, "Yeah, now! I'll share my coupon!"

With Kevin proposing such an offer, Deb schemed for a second, then said, "I'll tell you what, guys. If you all want to go now, Dad and I will go over and look at that bigger ship."

Tom was surprised by her suggestion, until he caught on. Their eyes met and they smiled naughtily.

Tom added, "I'll give you each ten more bucks if you keep an eye on each other. And if everyone gets to share Kevin's coupon. How would that be?"

Emily cheered, "Yes!"

Kevin said, "Aye!"

"Kaity, you stay close to Em," said Deb.

Kaitlyn saluted, "Aye, Aye!"

Tom dug into his wallet and handed Emily thirty dollars. "Meet us back at this spot in thirty minutes. Okay?"

The three kids ran off toward the Seaport entrance, near the gift shop. Kevin and Emily raced each other with Kaitlyn trying to keep up.

Kaitlyn cried, "Wait! You're making me hurry!"

Tom said to Deb, "You are bad."

Deb shrugged, "Of course. It's a list item."

"I'd forgot."

Deb teased playfully, "At least one of us is with the program. It's the Charles W. Morgan."

Tom remembered, "The oldest commercial ship, and the only wooden whaling ship left in the US. That's a damn good list item. Let's go add to its colorful, and soon to be sorted, history."

Tom and Deb stepped onto the deck of the Morgan, looking around at the fully restored piece of history. The enormous wooden ship was beautiful, with the booms, brackets, riggings and railings restored to a condition strong enough for a long sea voyage. Three huge white masts rose a hundred feet above the main deck toward the sky.

The deck was crowded with visitors of all ages. Tom and Deb now stood among them and watched the throngs move by. They both looked overwhelmed and anxious.

Tom said, "I don't know about this. There's a lot of people on this ship."

They walked across the main deck to a small, framed passage for access below deck. Looking down, there were steep wooden steps leading into the dark recesses of the ship. As Tom and Deb assessed this, a few other visitors congregated near them, waiting their turn to explore below.

Tom said, "I guess we should try here."

They turned around and, climbing backwards, descended the steps that were almost as steep as a vertical ladder.

The open, dark space of the lowest deck was full of tanks, crates and hydraulic systems forming a crowded, tangled aggregate. Narrow walkways allowed a handful of visitors, one at a time, to move slowly between the apparatuses.

Deb looked around, and said, "There's nowhere we can go for cover in here. It's just catwalks and machines."

On the level just above, the crew's deck, Tom and Deb were walking leisurely among other guests. They were holding hands, pretending to look at the trim and furnishings, and assessing the well-restored slice of Americana.

They stopped suddenly.

In front of them was an entrance to a network of connected spaces behind the near wall. There was only a pseudo-barrier to the entrance, a single thigh-high rope hung across the door frame. Inside were numerous triple-decker bunks, complete with small mattresses, pillows and privacy curtains. These were the crew's berths.

Deb whispered with excitement, "There are god damn beds in here! It's almost like a formal invitation!"

Tom was astonished. "What the heck! We must be at the right place!"

Tom looked over his shoulder. There was a volunteer, a young woman, near the steps where they had entered that deck. She was passively watching visitors mull around and was wearing an ID badge hung on a lanyard.

"There's a security person," Tom said with concern.

Deb turned to assess her. "She's just a volunteer."

Tom whispered, "Okay, we'll wait until no one is looking."

They inspected some wall maps and decorative wood trim much too carefully, for much too long, while constantly looking guiltily over their shoulders. The closest visitors to them, a young couple, with their arms around each other's waists, gave them an unconcerned look and walked further down.

The volunteer near the entrance was now explaining something to several members of a family crowded around her.

Tom urgently whispered, "Now!"

They both quickly stepped over the rope, and ducked behind the near wall.

Once they moved a little further inside the crew's quarters, they were out of sight of anyone else on board. There, it was darker, and there was a narrow passage between several sets of triple-decker bunks. The bunks were small, intended for men who were barely over five feet tall, and the privacy curtains didn't cover the openings very well. Tom and Deb slunk silently to the end, in front of the lowest bunk on the left, just above the floor.

A minute later, after they awkwardly and quietly crawled into the bunk, Tom slowly closed the privacy curtain.

The space inside the bunk was very cramped. Tom's full weight was almost crushing Deb, with the bottom of the next bunk flush against his head, his nose an inch from hers.

Deb said, in a strained, gasping whisper, "Maybe we should try front to back."

"Good idea."

Seven Minutes Later

At the edge of the berth space, one of Tom's eyes slowly peeked around the corner of the framed entrance. He stayed there for a second, then ducked back behind the wall.

He whispered, "The coast is clear."

Deb whispered, "I get it. Arjum."

He said, "Not arjum again! Shhhh!"

They quickly stepped from behind the wall, over the rope, then moved a few steps along the far wall. As they stood facing a hanging nautical picture, a middle-aged man standing there glanced at them with surprise. He had seen them exit the berth space.

Tom made eye contact with him with a guilty smile and asked, "How's it going?"

The man said, "I'm okay. Are we allowed to go in there?"

Tom sounded all professional. "Not normally, but we have authorization to be in there. We had to . . . appraise that area. It's on our list."

The man acted as if that made perfect sense and that he genuinely understood. While nodding, he said, "Your list. Sure, sure."

Without further comment, Tom and Deb quickly skulked along the wall, past the volunteer, and climbed the steps.

The Chandler family had reunited on the gravel road. The children were flaunting plastic bags from the gift shop.

Kaitlyn said with excitement, "I got a wooden puzzle, made by a ship builder that fixed the Morgan and the Amistad. He lives near here!"

Kevin said, "I got a great big magnifying glass!" Deb's mouth dropped open and Tom started to protest, but Kevin interrupted. "I promise, no more burning! I'll just look at bugs and stuff."

Emily said, "Thanks for the money. How was the Morgan, anyway?"

Tom made knowing eye contact with Deb. "It was very interesting, actually. Much better than we thought it would be."

Chapter 23

Sitting up in bed, Deb turned off the land line phone, looking visibly satisfied. She turned to Tom with a smile.

He had been listening and said, "That sounded promising."

"She's all settled in Sebring Pines, that senior community we visited when I was there in May. They have a great cognitive health center. The move went well, and she said everyone she's met so far is really nice."

Tom was afraid to ask, but did anyway. "And she actually agreed to give up her car?"

"Very reluctantly. Sebring has shuttle service to any service she might want. That Forester she has should sell pretty easily."

Tom sat up in bed. "That is a relief. I thought for sure she would put up a big fight about the car."

"The first day there, she got lost trying to get out of their parking lot. Get OUT of the parking lot. I think it was finally sinking in for her."

"How about the house? Is it going up for sale?"

"Not yet, it needs too much work, cleaning it out and fixing things. I'll have to go back sometime this summer to work on that. Get a real estate agent and contractors involved to assess what the house would need. Or maybe we can all take a field trip to Ohio for a few days."

Tom laughed. "The kids will love that. A dream vacation to northeastern Ohio."

"They haven't seen her for a couple years, and we can stay in a hotel. They'll like that. We'll probably just need to park a dumpster in the driveway and start throwing stuff in. Almost everything she hasn't taken to Sebring will get thrown in that, or given to Goodwill, or Habitat for Humanity. I'm sure Kevin especially will have a jolly good time chucking crap in a dumpster."

"I can't argue with that. Okay, we'll figure out a good time to do that."

"And get this. She already said when the house sells, we can have a big chunk of that money."

"Wow! Holy shit." Tom's mind immediately raced with the possibilities of extra money coming in to mitigate debt.

"Then she qualified the offer with, 'if it would help us out.'"

Tom laughed out loud.

Deb patted her heart, "Whoa. I was worried she was going to have a big meltdown. I'm so relieved it's off to a good start. One less thing to think about for now."

Deb leaned over for a hug and put her head on his chest. They lay down quietly together for quite a while.

Tom patted her shoulder, and said, only partially with sarcasm, "Let's just cuddle tonight."

Tom was standing at the front of the conference room, a projected graph on the whiteboard next to him. He used a laser pointer to highlight a key part of the slide.

"With the changes we've implemented, we are approaching maximum calculated efficiency of system performance. That is an increase of thirty percent resource utilization."

There was a shuffling of papers between Eric and Scott and muffled cries of excitement. They both had just notched a square on their bullshit bingo game sheets.

Ashley was sitting near the front of the table. She was all too aware of what they were doing, and she was not happy.

Looking back at them, she announced to the entire room, "Excuse me a second, Tom. Would everyone please make sure you understand how this was done. It's a good framework for actually working with management to improve processes, not just complain about them."

There was murmuring and stirring.

She then said, "Sorry to interrupt, Tom. Go ahead."

Eric and Scott attempted to hide their bingo sheets, then waited until she faced front. Eric turned to Scott, shielded his mouth from her view with a hand, stuck out his tongue, and flicked it rapidly up and down, imitating cunnilingus.

That evening, Tom arrived home from work and walked into the kitchen where Deb was cooking. A pan of stir-fried chicken and vegetables sizzled on the stove, the aroma filling the house. She turned to greet him.

"Hi Hun."

Tom was trying hard to stifle a huge grin. "Hey. That smells great."

Deb noticed his expression right away. "What's up with you?"

Tom's grin burst out without inhibition. "I've got a couple pieces of major scoopage."

"Scoopage? What is scoopage?"

"News flashes. Scoops. It's in Urban Dictionary. Just like your world famous 'arjum.'"

Deb quickly turned off the stove and moved the frying pan to a cold burner. She wiped her hands on the dish towel. "Tell me."

"You know we landed that huge government engine contract."

"Right. That was a couple weeks ago."

Tom said, "There's a celebration reception Friday for our department. Dinner, cocktails, a couple speeches. Significant others are invited."

"Fun. And I'm off that night."

"Perfect. Let's plan on that."

"Okay, great. What else?"

He said, "It's informal, at that place in Stonington, Dog Watch Cafe, I think."

Deb interrupted, "What other scoopage?"

Tom knew what she meant, hence his grin. "Oh, right." Smiling widely, he reached into his shirt pocket and pulled out a small envelope. He removed two tickets. "Ta-Da!"

"What's that?"

"Red Sox tickets for next Thursday night, against the Tigers."

Deb's immediate reaction was concern. "Did you buy those?"

Proudly he said, "SOEL season tickets, I got them for free. It was our department's turn. Ashley asked me if I wanted them, and after a femtosecond of deliberation, I said, 'sure.'"

"Very cool! And I don't have a gig that night!"

"I'll take the afternoon off. We can make a big date out of it."

Tom continued to grin, looking like the Cheshire Cat.

Her eyes narrowed, and she looked at him sideways. "What is it with you?"

"List item. Our grand finale. This could be our best chance."

Deb's eyes grew wide. "The seats are on the Green Monster?"

"No, they're box seats down the first base line, just past the Boston dugout."

Deb tried to figure it out. "There are so many other list items to do first. And it's supposed to be on the Monster."

"We'll have to figure out a way to do it on the Wall. And maybe the finale doesn't need to be the last thing. Just the most monumental, the Magnum Opus, the most dramatic, as you correctly pointed out at list inception."

Deb started to hesitate. "I don't, how . . ." Then she burst out with, "What the hell! I'm in, let's go for it. What have we got to lose?"

"We could get arrested. Or I could fall off the wall while climaxing and crush my spine like an accordion."

"That sounds so'r romantic. How could I say no?"

"You can't."

They hugged and kissed deeply, then slowly separated.

Tom said, "Mmm. And I am liking THIS list so'r much better than our first list."

Chapter 24

On the waterfront, a long wooden dock extended out into the rustic harbor and was crowded with moored sailboats and yachts. A modest, wood-sided restaurant was at the landward end next to an outside bar.

Having just secured a glass of white wine from that bar, Deb was standing alone on the dock, leaning against the wood railing, gazing longingly at the boats. She sipped the wine, which tasted fruity and dry, and breathed in the pleasant sea air. She sighed, happy for the moment of quiet.

Ashley's voice behind her asked, "Do you sail?"

Deb turned, surprised. Ashley approached the railing next to her. As they shook hands, Deb assessed her appearance, which was beautiful in an informal dinner dress. Deb also noticed she was drinking bottled water.

Deb beamed, "Hi Ashley! Good to see you again."

Ashley took a sip of water. "You too! Beautiful night, isn't it?"

"Kind of perfect. For mid summer, it's so comfortable. No, we've never had a chance to even try sailing. How about you?"

"Work and kids keep us pretty busy. Just like you, I'm sure."

Deb raised her glass. "Been there, done that, got the battle scars. Shouldn't you be celebrating? No cocktail tonight?"

Ashley looked away quickly. "Just water for me tonight. I, uh, have to say a few words later, and then drive home."

"Congratulations on the contract. That's huge for your department, isn't it?"

"Thanks, yes, it is. Hey, Tom mentioned you're looking for a position. There's a couple openings for senior admin assistants in Hydraulics."

Deb was surprised and said, "I am, thanks. What does a senior admin do?"

"More advanced assistant things. Scheduling site resources, like conference rooms, some light data entry and verification, occasionally some procurement and license renewals, things like that."

Deb said, "I can do that."

"If you're interested, check the company website. Tom can get you started, get you logged in with an account, and show you which positions to apply for."

Deb smiled, "I'll embellish, I mean, I'll update my resume this weekend."

Ashley laughed and said, "Frank Warren is the supervisor. I'll put in a good word for you. That'll speed up your application process."

Deb studied her, "Thanks, Ashley. That's very sweet of you."

She said sincerely, "No problem. Another Chandler at SOEL can only be a good thing. Your husband has been kicking ass the last few months. Keep feeding him whatever you've been feeding him."

Deb smiled knowingly, gave Ashley a wink, and raised her glass. "I promise I absolutely will."

A few minutes later, Tom and Deb were at the same railing with glasses of wine. A few other clusters of colleagues were chatting nearby.

Deb said, "Maybe you can look over my resume and help me polish it up. Make sure I highlight the right stuff and all that. And what I should include in the cover letter."

Tom took a sip of wine. "Of course. And I'll make sure you're at the right link for those jobs. I know Frank Warren, he's one of the good ones there."

"Ashley was so sweet," Deb said sincerely. "She really wanted to help."

"Yep. She actually is a good person. Just because she's smart and looks good, doesn't automatically make her a jerk, or even a slut."

Deb said mischievously, "Hmm. Smart and good-looking. I know someone else like that. He's not really a jerk, or even a slut. But he sure isn't a prude, either."

The following Thursday, Tom was in his cubicle, facing his monitors, concentrating hard, his fingers rapidly clacking on his keyboard.

Ashley came up behind him. "Tom, can I talk to you for a second?"

He spun his chair to face her, and stood. "Hi. Sure."

Tom followed Ashley down the row of cubicles. She stopped in an open space further down, away from other colleagues.

When they arrived there, she asked, "You're leaving for the rest of the week soon, right?"

"Yeah, the Sox game is tonight. I'm taking this afternoon and tomorrow off."

Ashley said seriously, "I wanted to let you know today, before you left. I just got word." Then she smiled broadly. "Your promotion went through. Senior Engineer."

Tom lit up, "Yes!"

He leaned forward to hug her, but Ashley leaned back and instead extended her hand. Then Tom realized they were in full view of colleagues, and that hugging wasn't the appropriate thing to do. Instead, he enthusiastically shook her hand.

Ashley beamed, "Congratulations!"

"Thanks!"

"Well-deserved. It goes into affect September first. Seven per cent increase in salary. You'll also get a bump in stock options and you'll start receiving a small annual allotment of RSUs. I'll get you the other info next week."

"Thank you so much for everything you had to do with it."

Ashley said, now a bit distracted, "I just documented how well you've been doing lately. I didn't do much of anything."

Tom was studying her. "There's something else, isn't there? I can tell. What is it?"

Ashley was flushed, but said, "One of your new responsibilities will be filling in for me as necessary, in some department matters. For example, early next year, when I'm out on maternity leave."

Tom said, "When you're . . ." Then it sunk in. "Oh my god! Yay!"

Tom lunged for a hug again. This time Ashley didn't stop him.

Chapter 25

The Volvo wagon was driving north on I-395 with almost no traffic. It was a clear, hot day.

"When's the interview?" Tom was driving, wearing a navy blue Red Sox cap and a New England Patriots jersey. 'BRADY' and '12' were on the back. Deb was wearing a pink Red Sox cap, a tight-fitting Boston tee shirt and a short black skirt. She removed two water bottles from a small back pack and placed them in the cup holders in the console.

She said, "Next week. I got an email from HR this morning. Your water is here in the front cupholder."

"Thanks. That was a pretty quick turn around for HR."

"I think Ashley had a lot to do with that." She opened her bottle, settled into her seat and took a swig. "It's hot."

"By game time it should be more comfortable."

Deb was thoughtful for a second, then asked, "So, how are we getting up to the Monster seats without tickets?"

"Doug's brother, Mike. He's an intern, mostly for ticket sales, but he does some VIP guest escorting in the park. That's allegedly what we will be. I have his cell number. I'll text him when we get there."

"He can just let us up there? Without tickets or a pass or something?"

Tom took a drink from his water bottle. "Doug said before the game it's okay to go on the wall with a staff escort. Mike will pretend we really are VIPs or something, I don't know. We'll just have to see what he says, then wing it."

Deb shook her head. "I really don't see pulling this off."

"Either way. We'll still have good seats for the game. For free." Tom glanced over and looked at her seriously. "I'm ready to try for our list finale. We'll just have to assess the dynamics of everything up there."

"'Assess the dynamics,'" she teased. "Listen to you, Mr. Fancy-Schmancy Engineer. Is that on one of those Bingo cards I've heard about?" She laughed, but then lightly fingered the hem of her skirt. "Do you recognize this?"

Tom looked down briefly, "One of your uniforms?"

"Exactly, a skirt. How often do I wear skirts, besides at work?"

"Um, never?"

"Give that man a prize. Yes, I'm ready, and I've planned ahead. I'll just have to get my panties off ahead of time, somehow."

"Clever girl." He thought for a second. "You might want to go to the rest room before we get up on the Wall."

She looked at him sideways, then took a long drink of water. "I'll make sure I need to go."

Tom and Deb were walking down crowded Lansdowne Street directly behind Fenway Park. To their right above, green steel beams angled over the sidewalk and street. An open parking deck and garage were to the left. Many vendors were selling food and souvenirs from tables and carts, yelling commentary about their selections to passing pedestrians. The smell of grilling meats, peppers and onions permeated the air. Traffic noise and voices echoed off steel and concrete.

Tom pointed to his left. "Sometimes long home runs that sail out of the park land on that parking deck. Cars get hit with balls a lot."

Deb said, "Why would anyone park there?"

"Well, it's convenient, that's for sure. And they would have a great story to tell. 'So-and-so's home run made this dent,' or something like that."

One of the vendors yelled at Tom. "Hey, Brady! How about a jersey for the right team?" He held up a Red Sox tee shirt. "He's not even in New England anymore!"

Tom yelled back, "I'm all set! Thanks anyway!"

Deb was looking up. "Is this actually the back of the Green Monster?"

Tom pointed up, "See those right angles in the cement? That is the actual bottom of the Monster Seats."

Deb pointed upward and said mischievously, "Oh, what we're going to do on you later."

There was a muffled blinging coming from Tom's shorts. He pulled his phone from a pocket.

He read the message out loud to Deb. "'Gate E, four forty-five.' Mike will meet us."

Deb looked at her phone. "It's four twenty. Where's Gate E?"

Tom walked to the middle of the street for a wider view. "Right back there."

"What should we do for half an hour?"

"There's a cool bar down further I want to show you. Let's get a beer."

The Bleacher Bar was crowded and noisy. Tom and Deb were holding beers carefully, slowly weaving around groups of patrons. They stopped at a metal railing near several fully seated tables.

Tom said, "Look out there."

Through a thick wire mesh on the closest wall, bathed in bright sunshine, were rust red dirt, luxurious green grass, and several baseball players. They were in red tee shirts and facing the other direction.

Deb said, "What is that? A practice field?"

"That's Fenway! This bar is actually in centerfield! Look, you can see the infield and batting cage way down, and the press boxes higher up."

Deb was straining to see. "Who are these players?"

"These are real Red Sox players, not animatronics. Probably mostly pitchers shagging batting practice fly balls."

Deb said with surprise, "It's right there, through the screen! We're on the field!"

He smiled, "I told you it was cool in here. We're right under the center field bleachers."

Deb took a sip of her beer, "We're missing practice?"

"The Tigers haven't practiced yet. Red Sox practice first at home. We can't get in the park this early."

Through the mesh and on the field, one of the players started running towards them, looking skyward over his shoulder. He slowed to a trot and stopped, looking in the direction of the bar. Just then, with a very loud clank, a baseball squarely hit the mesh, just a few feet from them.

Deb jumped, startled. Beer splashed from her glass, down her arm and to the floor. "Jesus! What the hell was that?"

The ball bounced away onto the dirt, and rolled back to the grass. The same player gloved it, turned and threw toward the infield.

Tom was laughing. "Better get used to it. On the Monster, balls could get hit right at us, without any protective screen to save us."

Deb switched the beer to her other hand and shook her wet fingers. "I'm so'r afraid."

Back down Lansdowne Street, at Gate E, Tom and Deb were waiting in a small crowd at a large door into Fenway. While Deb was people-watching, Tom was scrutinizing every person he could see in the park entrance.

She asked, "Do you know what he looks like?"

Tom continued to scan the crowd. "Doug said he looks like him. I met him quickly once."

"It's four-fifty."

Tom's gaze locked on one person. "I think that's him." Tom waved in recognition. "Yep, that's him. Let's go."

Inside the gate, cement, red brick and green painted steel constituted every structural surface. The crowd was sparse, but scattered people, in a wide diversity of shapes, colors and ages, constantly moved in all directions.

Mike Wilson looked like a slightly taller version of Doug. He was securing a purple wrist band on Deb. Tom was already wearing his.

Mike said, "As long as you have these on, you're good to go."

Tom asked with mild concern, "This won't get you in trouble?"

Mike said politely, but dismissively, "Not at all. I'm glad to do it. It's a PR thing. And Doug told me what a nice family Emily has."

"Aw, thanks" said Deb. "And it's okay even if we have tickets for somewhere else?"

Mike explained, "Here's how it works. I have to escort you up to the Monster Seats. During batting practice, there will be tour groups and lots of people coming and going up there."

Tom and Deb made concerned eye contact with each other.

Mike continued, "Once we get up there, I'll stay with you for a few minutes, and get you oriented. Then I have to get back to the phones. You can go in any of the Monster sections, unless there's a big tour group taking up the space."

Tom asked, "And we can just stay up there until the game starts?"

"No, until the general public is allowed in with their tickets. It's usually about five-forty. Then they'll kick everyone else off the Monster."

Tom asked, "Where's a good place to have a chance to catch batting practice balls, besides the Monster?"

Mike thought a second, "Down either line by the foul poles, or in straight-away center." He looked at Deb. "Sometimes flirting with the players will get a ball thrown to you."

"I'll leave that to her," laughed Tom.

"All set?" asked Mike. "Should we head up?"

Deb said quickly, "Uh, if you have a second, can I stop at the restroom first?"

"That's a good idea." Mike pointed, "There's a ladies room right there."

Tom said to Deb, "I thought you might need to make a pit stop."

Mike was studying them, having noticed their eye contact and interaction as they talked. "It must be nice to be married, and know someone that well."

Tom laughed, then imitated Newt in Aliens, "Mostly it's a nice thing, mostly."

Deb said as she turned, "I'll be right out."

As she was walking away, she glanced back and made mischievous eye contact with Tom.

Chapter 26

Forty feet above the field, from the top of the wall in the Monster Seats, the view of the park was glorious. Under the blue sky, the sun was slipping lower to the west, casting lengthening shadows across the perfectly manicured infield grass. The Detroit Tigers batting practice was in progress.

Mike finally said to Tom and Deb, "I'll head back to the offices. Are you guys all set?"

They were standing in the front row, taking in the view and watching batting practice. Several fans of all ages were on either side, including many children wearing baseball gloves, hoping to win the lottery by retrieving a ball. To their right, the heavy, crossed steel structure of the light tower rose above the wall like a skyscraper.

Tom said, "We're good, Mike. Thanks!"

"Hey, glad to do it," Mike said. "One of those ushers will tell you when you need to leave. Tell Emily I said hi." He turned to leave, but then added seriously, "Remember, pay attention. In batting practice, balls get hit up here a lot."

Deb called, "Thank you so much! We will!"

Mike shuffled past several fans, then climbed the first set of steps until he was out of sight.

Deb watched him leave. "We should get him something as a thank you."

A slight, frail elderly man, Murray Rosen, caught sight of Deb as she was speaking. He gave her a cool, appraising once-over, looking at her legs for much too long. Slowly, he moved closer to her, pretending it was just by circumstance, and to 'casually check out the view.'

When Murray was near, he said to Deb, "I've been coming to Fenway for sixty-nine years. And this is my first time up here.

It used to be just a net, you know. Workers had to climb a ladder to get up here to get home run balls."

Deb said, "It's a wonderful view, isn't it?"

On the other side of him, Mrs. Rosen had moved closer and was annoyed. In a screeching, nagging tone, she said, "Murray, leave her alone!"

"Oh, he's fine," said Deb. "I don't mind."

Mrs. Rosen shook her head and added, not very subtlety, "He's always flirting with pretty, young women. I just don't know what he expects to happen!"

Murray ignored her and asked, "Are your seats in this row?"

Deb said, "Oh no, we're just up here to . . . enjoy the view for a few minutes. We're sitting way down by the dugout."

Mrs. Rosen screeched, "Murray, get over here right now!"

Murray rolled his eyes and slowly moved away. "Well, have a good time, Miss."

"Thanks! You too!"

Tom was looking around behind them but then leaned closer to Deb and said quietly, "You pretty young thing. We have to make damn sure we don't become like them, in thirty or forty years."

"It is a goal to strive for."

"Let's make it a vow. We can do a pinky swear later."

Tom walked up a step, and scoped out the layout of the Monster Seats to their right, then to their left. The front row was crowded. The only two security men were on the steps to their left, wearing red shirts and ID badges on lanyards around their necks. A few fans were standing in the second row, near the light tower.

When Tom turned back toward the field to watch practice, his gaze suddenly moved up. He called out loudly, "Heads up!"

He moved quickly to the right. Extending his arm outward in a token gesture, he continued to gaze skyward, his eyes following the path of something.

Suddenly, a baseball clanked loudly off the light tower, fifteen feet above the front row, rattled around in the steel, then fell fifty feet to the field below.

Several children on the wall immediately yelled to the players down on the field, "Throw it here! Throw it here!"

A Tiger player grabbed the ball, and without so much as a glance up at the kids, threw it back towards the infield. A loud chorus of boos rose from the kids, and other fans.

Tom had been watching and was amused by the whole event. He turned back to face the light tower. Up the steps along the tower foundation, there was a wall blocking access to the space underneath. Tom walked up the steps to the third row and turned to the right. No one at all was in that row.

He evaluated the number of people near the light tower wall, behind him, further down his row, then to the front. His gaze shifted to Deb, who was still among the fans watching batting practice in the front row. In a few seconds she made eye contact with him, and he nodded for her to join him. She walked across the front row and climbed the steps to him.

Tom said when she arrived, "Just stand here a second."

"What are you thinking?" She thoughtfully assessed each location as he described them.

"Look," he said, "this wall below the tower blocks the view completely this way. That way, there's no one in this row for three sections. I bet if we get down between seats over here, we'll be out of sight."

Deb ran through a scheme in her mind. "Let me try something." She looked around, pretending to be surprised. Then, not too loudly, she said, "Lordy! I do believe I've dropped my serviette!" She stooped to her knees and crouched below the front wall of their row. She then shuffled forward between two seats, moving up as far as she could fit.

Tom asked quietly, "Can you see anyone?"

"No. Not even the people down three sections."

Tom said anxiously, "Uh oh. Are we really going to do this?"

Deb grabbed the seat closest to Tom and swiveled it toward him. "Sit here a second."

Tom apprehensively sat down and rotated the seat toward her. She immediately started to rub the crotch of his shorts.

Tom urgently said, "What are you doing?"

Deb whispered, "When we start, you'll have to be ready to go! No time for foreplay! This is important business!"

Tom realized she was right, and asked, "Are you ready?"

She yanked open her small bag and tilted it toward him, revealing her white panties balled up inside. "I'm ready."

She rubbed him again.

Tom said quietly, "Oh . . . my . . . god."

She said, "We'll just . . ." But felt the lump in his shorts growing quickly. "Oh my, this isn't taking long."

From the seats in front of them, as he sat behind the wall of their row, Tom was only visible from the chest up. He was looking from side to side rapidly, obviously nervous.

Barely in a whisper, he said, "Oh god. I'm ready."

Deb stopped rubbing and got on her knees, facing away from the light tower. Tom dropped from the seat to his knees behind her and unbuckled his shorts and slid them down. Just then, there was an obvious increase in the volume of cheering emanating from the fans in the front row. He did not know why, but he was pretty sure it wasn't because he had lowered his shorts.

A second later, in their row a few feet from them, a baseball hit the back wall with a very loud, BANG! It bounced off the floor with a thud, and ricocheted off a seat back. It then flew straight up into the air, a few feet from where they were kneeling.

Tom, with his shorts down, and Deb, with her butt exposed, watched the ball in horror, not daring to breath.

As if happening in super slow motion, the ball landed hard on the shelf of their row. It bounced twice, then seemed to hang in the air interminably. It was not clear which way it was going to fall.

It bounced again, landed on the lip of the shelf, then fell over the front wall, out of their sight and into the next row.

Tom and Deb remained frozen as there was a flurry of footfalls and yelling in the next row. Then, there was a loud thunk against the wall directly on the other side from them.

Just then a boy yelled triumphantly, "I got it! I got it!" followed by various groans of disappointment.

Tom was wincing while tensely waiting, looking down the row for anyone moving their way.

A few seconds passed. Footfalls and cheering quickly faded.

Deb said, over her shoulder, "Better get going. It's now or never."

Tom's shorts fell the rest of the way to his calves on the cement, quickly followed by his white jockey shorts.

Murray Rosen was slowly walking up the steps on the Green Monster, just passing the second row. At the third row, he stopped and gazed to his left, catching sight of something moving. Soon Deb was in view, on her hands and knees, the top of her pink cap visible with her head bent down. She was rocking back and forth slightly.

Murray was looking down the row at her, first with concern, then with piqued interest when he realized it was Deb. Then, with widening eyes and great interest. Mrs. Rosen was just behind him.

Mrs. Rosen nagged, "Why are you stopping?"

Murray called to Deb, "Are you okay, Miss?"

Deb looked up, horrified, eyes wide. Tom tried to duck down out of sight, but he was quite visible.

Deb gasped, struggling to speak. "Oh, yes. I'm just . . . looking for my contact lens. It just popped right out!"

Rosen nodded. Of course, that seemed very obvious now. "Do you need any help?"

She said loudly, much too quickly, "No! No, I think I see it. Yes, I've got it." She pretended to pick up her nonexistent contact lens. "Thanks, though!"

Rosen waved and resumed walking slowly up the steps, while watching her continuously.

Mrs. Rosen followed, now looking their way. She frowned, but also watched until she was out of sight, past the front wall of the next row.

Deb said urgently, over her shoulder, "How's it going back there?"

Tom began grunting quietly again, "One . . . more . . . minute."

Deb closed her eyes, put her head down, and rocked slightly.

Suddenly her mouth and eyes opened and her expression changed to surprise as she turned and looked back. Tom groaned softly. Deb closed her eyes and smiled, ever so slightly, while thinking, pièce de résistance!

Five Hours Later

The game was in progress under the lights. The stands were jam-packed throughout the entire park.

Tom and Deb were standing at their seats in the overflowing box section down the first base line. Crowd noise was at a fevered pitch as all fans around them were screaming and clapping.

Deb yelled to Tom, though he was right next to her, "Who's up?"

Tom called, "Xander! We just need one more hit and it's a walk off!"

The bases were full of Red Sox runners in their white uniforms. Tiger players in gray uniforms were in the field. The sea of fans filling the stands were in constant motion like a shimmering red and blue hillside moving in the wind.

On the mound, the pitcher came to the set, wound up quickly, and threw.

Xander swung and made solid contact with a resounding, crack!

The ball rocketed out on a hard, straight line, landing on the grass in left center field and skittering up against the Green Monster. The outfielders quickly gave up as there was nothing they could do.

Tom and Deb leapt with their hands in the air as the crowd exploded into cheers, reaching a deafening crescendo.

On the field, Red Sox players rushed from the dugout and swarmed near first base, around Xander. It became a frenzied, joyous scrum to end the game with a win.

Approaching midnight, Tom was driving on the Massachusetts Turnpike, looking tired but very content. He glanced to his right for a bit too long, then smiled, even more content.

Deb was sitting sideways facing him, her eyes closed. The indirect light from headlights and the dashboard gave her face a radiant glow.

Her eyes suddenly opened and she looked up at Tom. She asked quietly, "What are you looking at?"

"You caught me. I was just noticing how pretty you are, just like your best buddy Murray's wife said."

Deb closed her eyes. "Mmm, thanks. But don't think your flattery will get me to do that at a Patriots game."

"As long as your contact lens isn't scratched, I'm happy."

She smiled widely. "It was the best I could come up with, you know, quick thinking on my feet."

"You weren't on your feet, young lady. But it was a very good save."

"Thanks." She closed her eyes, still smiling. "And don't think I don't know that the Patriots season starts in a few weeks. Don't even think about that. It's not on the list."

"Damn. Well, then, maybe we should . . . take a flight somewhere for our next outing."

"A flight to where?"

Tom laughed, "Where we go doesn't matter. Getting there will be the, uh, adventurous part."

They both laughed as Tom reached across and held her hand.

Chapter 27

The waterfront restaurant was in an absolutely beautiful setting on a small harbor in the quaint, New England village. Anchored sailboats crowded the water just off shore. Gulls squawked and dipped around the buildings and boats, while several cormorants stood perched on rocks or posts.

The Chandlers were seated at a round wooden table under a large umbrella on the planked exterior deck. A split wood railing formed an open barrier to the water behind them, not far from their table.

Tom was facing the water, with Deb sitting next to him. Emily, Doug, Kevin and Kaitlyn were seated around the table. Bright sunlight, from a low angle in the sky, danced over the water and shone across their open menus and place settings.

Kaitlyn asked Deb, "What can we order?"

"Anything you want, sweetie."

Kaitlyn got very excited. "Even fried clams?"

"Of course! And we can even order dessert after."

"Wow! I'm starved! I can't wait for my food!" said Kevin. "Can I get a lobster roll, and French fries? They're like twenty-three dollars!"

Tom said, "Yes, you can. That's what I'm getting. We're celebrating, so everyone get whatever you want!"

Doug said, "Thanks Mr. C, that sounds great. I think I'll get a hot lobster roll, too."

After the waitress took their orders, the family chatted happily for twenty minutes, and gazed at boats coming and going. Kevin and Kaitlyn had left their seats and stood at the railing, looking for anything interesting in the water. They watched boats gliding and rocking, birds soaring and dipping, and kept an eye out for seals in the water.

While Kevin and Kaitlyn were still at the railing enjoying the scene, the waitress brought a large tray holding all their meals. She set it down on a small table near the railing to distribute the plates. First, she picked up two lobster roll dinners and carried them the few steps to the table. Seeing Kevin wasn't there, she laid those dinners in front of Doug and Tom.

Deb called, "Kaity, Kevin, food's here!"

Suddenly, Tom caught sight of movement in the sky above them, coming from over the water. A gull was swooping in quickly toward the unattended, unprotected tray of dinners near the railing.

Without time to think, Tom burst out in knee-jerk reaction, "Look out! Look out!"

But before anyone else knew what was happening, the gull grabbed the entire remaining lobster roll in its bill and swooped up and away. With amazing deftness, it did not drop a single chunk of lobster. Everyone, including the waitress, stood a bit in shock as it happened quickly and was all over in three seconds.

Just as Kevin got to the table, he saw the gull fly away, and then saw that Doug and Tom already had their rolls. He cried, "Was that my lobster roll?" He immediately appeared to be on the verge of tears.

Deb said quickly, "Don't worry, Kevin, she'll bring another roll for you."

The waitress looked panicked at first but said, "I am so sorry! I'll bring another one right out!" She quickly distributed the other dinners and hurried back to the kitchen.

Tom placed his plate in front of Kevin. "Here, buddy, I haven't touched this. You can have mine."

Kevin immediately perked up. "Thanks, Dad."

Deb teased Tom, "'Look out, look out?' What are you, the Leader of the Pack?"

Emily and Doug were trying hard not to laugh, and Emily said, "Yeah, Dad, it wasn't exactly obvious what that meant."

"Well, sorry, I wasn't quite prepared for how to deal with a lobster-stealing seagull."

A half hour later, everyone had finished their meals. Kevin, in particular, had enjoyed his lobster roll. An open bottle of champagne was chilling in ice near Tom, and partially filled glasses of champagne were at each setting. Kaitlyn's and Kevin's glasses had just enough for one sip.

Deb said to Tom, "You ready?"

He said to everyone, "Guys, I'd like to propose a toast."

Each of them raised their champagne glasses. Kaitlyn and Kevin, who were particularly excited, looked at each other and giggled. They knew they were getting away with something.

Tom raised his glass and looked directly at Deb. "First, to Mom, for getting her new job. She starts in a couple weeks."

Deb was smiling sheepishly, a look of some relief.

Emily cheered, "Yay, Mom!"

Tom said, "No more late nights and weekends!"

Deb cheerfully said, "Hooray!" She raised her glass higher. "And to Dad's promotion! He's worked so hard to get it. It will help us all!"

Kevin called, "Yippee!"

"To Dad!" said Emily.

"Thanks, everyone." Tom paused, looked down for a second, and spoke with a more serious tone. "I also want to propose a toast to our whole family. To you all for being such great kids. Maybe there's a little drama here and there," he looked at Kevin, "but you all work hard in school, and have been helping out when Mom and I have been so busy. And being responsible so we could get away for our little trips. It helped Mom and me so much."

Moving his arm around the table, Tom raised his glass to each of them, and sipped his champagne. He then looked directly at Deb.

He continued with, "And especially to Mom. It's been tough for us sometimes, but you've always worked so hard. This year, spending more quality time with you, I realized so clearly, how much I do love you."

Emily gushed, "Awwww!"

Kevin's face scrunched up. "Mushy stuff."

"Thanks," said Deb. "I love you, too. So much."

They leaned across the edge of the table and kissed.

Kaitlyn covered her eyes.

Tom got a bit choked up. "What a wonderful family we have."

Deb agreed, "We sure do."

Then Tom remembered something else. "Hey, everyone. There's a few weeks left before school, and before Mom starts her new job. How about if we all take a little vacation together? Maybe a long weekend somewhere?"

Kevin piped up, "Cool!"

"Where can we go?" asked Kaitlyn.

Emily quickly offered, "New York! Finally, we can go to Broadway!"

Kevin said, "A cruise on a boat!"

Kaitlyn said, "A beach house! I want to see Cape Cod."

Tom held up his hands, "Hold it, hold it. Hun, what do you think?"

Deb considered briefly. "How about if we each write down our top three choices, put them all together, and figure out what we all want to do the most?"

Tom was startled. He said measuredly, "You mean, make a list?"

Deb's mouth dropped open. "Yes, I think making a list is exactly what I mean."

Tom nodded his head. "A list is good. I am definitely comfortable working off a list."

Emily was staring at them, shaking her head. She finally said, "What in the world are you two talking about?"

THE END

Lawrence M. Zaccaro

Mr. Zaccaro was a research biologist, negotiated legal contracts for a major pharmaceutical company, and taught college science courses. He has developed a family card game called Wordplay, has written a children's book, Amy and the Orca, and a science fiction novel, Convergent. He is a proud father and grandfather and lives in Connecticut. Mr. Zaccaro may be contacted for signing or speaking engagements at: zaccarolarry@gmail.com

Cover designed and illustrated by

Patrick Regan

pat123xyz.com

Made in the USA
Middletown, DE
18 February 2022

61124102R00092